THE BILLIONAIRE'S SIREN

HEART AND SOUL

S.E. SMITH

ACKNOWLEDGMENTS

I would like to thank my husband, Steve, for believing in me and being proud enough of me to give me the courage to follow my dream. I would also like to give a special thank you to my sister and best friend, Linda, who not only encouraged me to write, but who also read the manuscript. Also, to my other friends who believe in me: Julie, Jackie, Christel, Sally, Jolanda, Lisa, Laurelle, Debbie, and Narelle. The girls that keep me going!

And a special thanks to Paul Heitsch, David Brenin, Samantha Cook, Suzanne Elise Freeman, PJ Ochlan, Vincent Fallow, L. Sophie Helbig, and Hope Newhouse, Allison River, Jonathan Strait, and Bethanne Reid—the outstanding voices behind my audiobooks!

    – S. E. Smith

Contemporary Romance
THE BILLIONAIRE'S SIREN
S.E. Smith Signature Romance: Heart & Soul series
Copyright © 2025 by S.E. Smith
First E-Book Published August 2025
Cover Design by Laurelle Santamaria

Summary: She has a past she won't share. He has a future he wants to build with her. But when passion collides with secrets, can love survive?

ISBN: 978-1-963823-77-6 (Paperback)
ISBN: 978-1-963823-76-9 (eBook)
ISBN: 978-1-963823-81-3 (Hardcover)

Romance | Contemporary | Action/Adventure | Enemies to Lovers | Billionaire | International | Hidden Identity

Published by Montana Publishing, LLC & SE Smith of Florida Inc. www.sesmithfl.com

 Formatted with Vellum

SYNOPSIS

He offered her a fortune for a night...

Greek billionaire Alexandros Kallistratos is knocked to his knees—literally—when he encounters a furious, auburn-haired siren who has been locked in his private stateroom aboard his yacht. Before he can demand answers, she does the improbable—she jumps overboard to escape him.

But fate isn't finished with them yet.

Danika "Dani" Collins is no mermaid... just a fiercely independent marine mechanic with secrets she's not ready to share—especially not with the dangerously tempting Greek who dove into the sea after her.

Fascinated by the woman who refuses his generous offer for a night in his bed, Alexandros isn't above using a little enchantment of his own to win her over. But Dani is unimpressed by his wealth, unmoved by his name... but undeniably drawn to his kisses.

What Dani fears more than surrendering to his touch is losing her heart. Because love comes with a cost—and her past is more dangerous than Alexandros realizes.

He'll do anything to protect her. Claiming Dani means risking it all… especially once he discovers she's carrying their future, but will she be willing to give their love a chance?

CHAPTER 1

"*S*on of a hairy ant's belly."

Dani Collins's curse was muffled by the pad of her thumb as she sucked on her bleeding finger. The sharp sting bit deeper than her pride, but only just. She glared down at the broken nail file in her lap—an outdated, half-rusted relic she'd fished from the back of the vanity drawer. It wasn't much, but in the war of lock versus mechanic, it had been her only weapon.

Around her, the cabin oozed obscene elegance, like someone had taken a five-star hotel and smooshed it into a floating palace. The floor beneath her bare feet was a swirling expanse of creamy travertine marble, cool and polished to a mirror-like sheen. A plush, navy-blue area rug—likely silk—spread across the center like a velvet sea, its intricate Greek key pattern gleaming with faint threads of gold.

To her left, a wall of smoked glass held back a gleaming mini-bar stocked with crystal decanters and top-shelf liquor, all perfectly backlit like museum pieces. Above it, recessed lighting glowed from a coffered ceiling painted in soft ivory, throwing golden halos across the crown molding. Even the air smelled expensive—like sea salt and leather with a hint of overpriced cologne.

The bed behind her was an oversized monstrosity wrapped in

cream Egyptian cotton sheets and more throw pillows than any human could ever justify. A hand-carved headboard loomed behind it, made of the same high-gloss mahogany as the curved wall panels and the door she now stared at with a mix of hope and fury.

Through that very door—solid, thick, and smug with its gleaming brass hardware—she could hear music thumping louder now. Jazz mixed with something electronic. A saxophone wailing like it had drunk too much champagne. Laughter, clinking glasses, and the occasional squeal of drunken delight floated toward her, accompanied by the sweet, sour scent of hors d'oeuvres and perfume.

She tilted her head, listening. Yep. The party was in full swing. Vito Marino's ego-fest had officially launched.

"I hope that little prick has a miserable time," she muttered, adjusting her sore shoulder with a wince. *"Come, let me show you around,"* she added in a mocking singsong, mimicking Vito's greasy charm. "I should never have fixed his blasted engine. That's another thing I'll take care of when I get out of here. I'm going to tear it apart and dump the pieces all over his pretty little yacht in places he'll never find."

She leaned back on her calves and exhaled slowly. Between the dazzling light fixtures that looked like inverted crystal fountains and the silent hum of wealth around her, it was easy to feel out of place—even if she hadn't been locked in a glorified jewelry box.

"Who puts an electronic lock on a boat door?" she hissed. "What if the damn boat sinks? Rich idiots. That's what they are. Designer-suited, over-sprayed tans, selfie-snapping—"

Snap.

The nail file broke again, this time into a piece too small to salvage, with a pitiful *ting*. The jagged end clattered to the marble floor like a dropped sword in the final round.

Dani stared at the shard, her eye twitching. "Unbelievable."

She dropped her head against the heavy mahogany door with a soft thud, letting the chill of the polished wood seep into her forehead. Her breath came in shallow spurts now, a mix of frustration, adrenaline, and the creeping edge of panic she'd been fighting to ignore for the last hour and a half.

"Stupid... potato heads," she muttered, her voice muffled against the door. "You don't lock a door on a boat. You don't lock a door on a boat. What if it sinks? What if there's a fire? What if—?"

Her mind raced with increasingly dramatic scenarios, none of them helpful. Trapped in a glorified shoebox, on a yacht owned by a man with all the integrity of a used car commercial, with nothing but a broken nail file and a questionable pillow for defense.

She was going to die in here. Dressed like a sparkly tomato, smelling like champagne, and with glitter stuck to parts of her body that she didn't even want to think about.

Her groan was stifled when a faint sound pierced through the bubble of her despair—footsteps.

Soft. Confident. Approaching.

Dani's head jerked up. Her heart leapt to life like a car engine catching after the third crank. Hope rocketed through her chest.

She leaned forward, pressing her ear to the door. Yes, those were definitely footsteps. Raising her hands, she pounded with both hands, her palms slapping against the wood in a frantic rhythm.

"Help! Hey—HEY! I'm in here! Open the door! Please!"

She drove her shoulder against it, more to make noise than anything. Her voice cracked with rising desperation.

"Oh, for the love of—will someone please open this dang—"

The footsteps paused. Dani pressed her ear to the door again, holding her breath. Suddenly, the electronic lock made a beeping sound before the door slid open.

Dani blinked. Air sucked into her lungs. She was still on her knees. All she could see was the expensive sheen of tailored black slacks and the sculpted knees beneath.

"Ti sto THEE-a-o-lo?—?" *What the hell?!*

Oh, thank God. Oh, crap. What if it's Vito?

Without thinking, without looking, Dani snapped into survival mode.

Her fist shot out like a piston, a perfect uppercut to the unprotected terrain of the man's groin.

A strangled sound erupted above her—a hiss, followed by a breathless groan that might've made her wince... if she hadn't already launched herself up like a rocket.

She bolted, clutching her boots in one hand, red gown flaring around her legs like a cape as she rammed her shoulder into her poor, unfortunate rescuer.

The man staggered back against the gleaming mahogany wall with a solid thud. "Ah, *gamoto*—!" he grunted, his voice hoarse and guttural.

Not waiting for a second round, Dani took off down the corridor.

Run, Dani, run!

The hilarious comedic line flashed through her mind as she ran, causing her to stumble as an adrenaline-fueled snort of giggles slipped from her.

Plush carpet silenced her bare feet as she sprinted past antique brass sconces and decorative alcoves filled with sculptures that cost way more than her Vespa. The corridor felt endless—curved walls and soft lighting designed to lull the wealthy into a champagne-fueled haze.

But she wasn't sipping bubbly. She was making a mad dash for freedom.

Behind her, a furious volley of curses and shouts, demanding she halt, filled the air. The curses were in Greek. The orders to halt were in a mix of Greek, English, and Italian. She had to admit she was impressed with his range of knowledge of multiple languages. None of them were easy to learn.

She also noted that none of the curses were flattering, and all of them were terse with anger.

A glance over her shoulder showed the man wasn't giving up.

She swerved, dodged a steward with a tray of shrimp cocktail, and hit the staircase two steps at a time, praying her legs didn't give out before she reached open air.

Freedom. She just needed to reach the deck.

"Ms. Collins! Dani!"

Dani winced at the sound of her name slicing through the music—and not in a good way, like a smooth DJ transition. No, this was more like a needle-skipping-across-vinyl moment, and it was aimed squarely at her.

She burst through the arched, gold-inlaid doorway and onto the upper deck like a cannonball of chaos hurled at a royal gala.

Instant silence rippled outward from her entrance. Conversations halted. Champagne glasses froze mid-air. One woman with a diamond choker large enough to fund a small nation blinked, uncertain if she was witnessing a mental breakdown, a social experiment, or both.

Dani didn't care. She had bigger problems. Namely, the huge guy charging behind her. From the crash of metal and the loud expletives, he hadn't been as nimble as her. Her sympathies went to the poor bloke who would be picking pieces of shrimp out of the carpet. The smell would be a bear to get rid of, not to mention the stains.

"He can afford it. No sympathies, Dani," she muttered, veering in the opposite direction of Vito's voice.

She could imagine just what her entrance into the posh occasion must look like. Her sequined red gown was barely clinging to her body. She hadn't zipped it. The spaghetti-string straps holding the bodice drooped dangerously low, held up only by sheer willpower, desperation, and the help of her black, cotton sports bra.

Her hair—previously doused in champagne and cleaned with a quick shampoo in the shower before she realized Vito's amorous intentions—had dried into a medusa-like halo of curls that swayed with each furious step she took. Her bare feet padded across the plush carpeted salon. She clutched her grimy, steel-toe work boots like twin weapons of mechanical justice.

A steward blinked as she stomped past him, gently rotating his silver tray so the foie gras didn't slide off. The waitstaff exchanged sidelong glances of bemused alarm, but none stepped in. Clearly, this wasn't their first yacht drama.

Dani frantically scanned the crowd as she walked—no, stormed—

across the inner salon, her expression a mixture of righteous fury and 'I'm two seconds away from lighting this whole damn boat on fire.'

"Dani!" Vito's voice, syrupy and panicked, slithered over the crowd.

Her eyes locked on him—tan, oily, and far too smug for a man who had locked her in a glorified dressing room. He stood near a group of glamorous guests beside the piano, holding a flute of Dom Pérignon like it was an Oscar. His cologne reached her before he did.

"I can explain," he said, flashing a sheepish grin that probably worked on drunken heiresses but only made Dani want to throw a shoe.

"Yeah?" she snapped, holding up one boot. "How about I explain my feelings… with a steel-toe demonstration?"

A collective gasp swept through the crowd as her voice—definitely not demure or dulcet—rang out like a rallying cry. One elderly gentleman snickered and was elbowed by his companion while a woman in a glittering silver dress choked on her shrimp canapé.

Dani was feeling pretty confident until she looked back the way she had come. From the lower deck stairs, *he* emerged. Her accidental victim. Her very furious, very male, very intimidating victim.

And now she could really see him.

"Oh, for crying out loud!" she groaned skyward when she felt an instant attraction sweep through her. "Give me a frigging break up there, please!"

If the heavens were listening, they weren't being generous. No, there looked like there would be some serious retribution in store for her if she wasn't fast enough to escape it.

Tall, broad-shouldered, and carved like a Greek tragedy, the man moved with a lethal grace. He didn't run—he hunted. And at the moment, he was hunting her.

His jaw was sharp enough to cut diamonds, his cheekbones angled just right to make sculptors weep, and his dark eyes… oh, those eyes.

Not brown. Black coffee before a storm kind of eyes.

And they were locked onto her like a heat-seeking missile.

Is that murder I see reflected at me? her brain whispered with a laugh.

Her instincts shrieked: *Run, you idiot!*

Her entire body jolted in agreement as the space between her and the two men shrank. On one side, seduction. On the other, divine retribution.

A hush fell again, as if everyone knew a reckoning was at hand.

Dani felt heat creep up her neck. Not from shame, no—she had passed the exit ramp to shame a couple of hours ago. No, this was from the absolutely unacceptable twinge of attraction at seeing the guy she'd just nut-punched in an expensive hallway.

Eyes flicked from her to him, to Vito stalking towards her, and back again, like the world's wealthiest tennis match.

Crap. That is new.

"Stop! Now!" the Greek God ordered.

"When Zeus becomes a monk!" she shot back.

She wasn't giving up. Freedom was only one leap away.

But so was he.

Dani wasn't entirely sure which one was more dangerous.

The slimeball who had wanted to charm her into oblivion with a vat of cologne and his "sweetheart" routine…

…or the tall, Greek thundercloud who was stalking toward her like he'd stepped out of Mount Olympus with vengeance on his mind and a vendetta lodged somewhere between his clenched teeth.

Maybe it hadn't been a good idea to use his family jewels for a punching bag, she reluctantly conceded.

"Dani! Sweetheart, let us go back downstairs and discuss this misunderstanding," Vito cooed over the now-muted music, his voice honeyed and thick with false concern.

Dani's head whipped toward the voice that made her stomach churn.

Dani caught the expression in Vito's eyes—hungry, entitled, and heated in the worst way. The look that made her skin crawl and her fight-or-flight instincts scream like an air-raid siren.

"That's never going to happen unless it is to hide your dead body," she swore, shooting daggers at Vito.

Out of her peripheral vision, Dani saw her window of opportunity open. A steward was entering through a set of sliding doors that led to the side deck. If she remembered right, it looped around toward the stern. A potential escape route. Possibly. Hopefully.

Behind her, she heard the low snarl of her nemesis—not Vito, no, the other one. The tall, chiseled man she'd wronged with enthusiastic precision.

She pushed through, startling the steward balancing the silver tray laden with high-end appetizers. Dani zig-zagged, snatched a handful of whatever was nearest on the tray, and stuffed it in her mouth—*food is fuel, food is fuel*—only to gag as the texture hit her.

Caviar. Slimy, salty, overpriced fish pudding.

She gagged again, spit it out in her hand, and instinctively flung the offending mess over her shoulder. A satisfying splat and a loud Greek curse followed.

She paused, just long enough to glance back—and burst into a short, snorting laugh.

Her furious stalker had just taken a direct hit to the face. Bits of caviar clung to the stubble on his cheek like glittering seaweed. His face was a mask of stunned disbelief even as the growing twitch in his jaw promised future consequences, but for now, Dani took the win.

"Sorry about that," she said breezily. "Should've gone with the shrimp."

With a snort of laughter, she turned and ran.

She launched herself down the curved steps leading toward the outer deck. The wind, which had picked up a little since earlier, caught at the loose folds of her gown. The thin material slipped down over her full breasts again, barely clinging to her curves. She gripped it, holding a death grip on the neckline. Her boots slapped against her thigh, still tied together and swinging like she was wielding a medieval flail.

The music faded behind her. The sea air hit her like a slap of reality—sharp, fresh, and warm against her damp skin. She stumbled off the last step and landed on the lower deck on her knees, wincing when they collided with the polished teak. Her breath came in bursts of short, hard gasps.

Ahead, the Mediterranean stretched out in endless indigo shimmer before her. The shoreline sparkled a few hundred yards away, like a promise she wasn't supposed to reach.

The *Kallistratos Challenge* was no longer docked.

"Perfect," Dani muttered, struggling to her feet. "Just... flipping... perfect."

The opulent yacht was anchored offshore—probably to keep out party-crashers. The irony made her laugh, breathless and hysterical.

"Alrighty then," she whispered, eyeing the lifeboat housing on the port stern. It was low enough. If she aimed right, she'd miss the propellers and not break a bone.

Hopefully.

She tugged the sagging gown up, gripping the hem in one fist and hoisting it above her knees. Her boots were still looped over her arm. She clutched them tighter, testing the jump with a glance and a deep inhale. She needed to move closer to the stern—and lower if possible.

"I'm not stupid," she told herself aloud.

Well... not always.

But she was definitely daring.

Without waiting another second, Dani descended a second set of steps. Above her, she could already hear footsteps pounding toward her. Shouts. The thud of something—someone—hitting the wall she'd flown past.

Too late.

Dani landed with a soft thud on the lower deck, nearly toppling forward again as her feet hit the polished teak. She stumbled, righted herself, and pulled the red gown higher where it had slipped danger-ously low, tucking it under her arm along with her boots.

The sea stretched out before her—dark, glittering, beautiful.

It would be a challenging swim to the dock. She calculated she could make it in fifteen, maybe twenty minutes. She wasn't worried about that. She could do twice that distance if pushed. The only thing that made her stomach clench was the thought of leaving her tool bag behind.

Her poor, beautiful baby. She had no idea where it was now.

Likely being used as a footrest by Vito or, worse, stuffed in a broom closet next to his ego.

"Stop! Now!"

The barked command sliced through the night, sharp and domineering.

Dani twisted, her breath catching as she took a slow step backward. Mesmerized by the thought of her escape, she had given her pursuer time to catch up with her. For a second, she wondered if she had done it on purpose—so she could see him one last time.

With an exasperated shake of her head at her wayward thoughts, she scowled and moved backwards. She curled her toes against the smooth deck as she turned to face her pursuer.

A shaft of moonlight illuminated his face—and she promptly decided she had made at least three poor life choices tonight, starting with accepting the job and ending with punching the wrong man.

Yep, I'm dead.

That was the only way to summarize the expression carved into the man's face. His jaw, sculpted and sharp, was clenched so tightly it could've shattered diamonds. His black hair was tousled in a way that looked unintentional, but was somehow more devastating for it. And those eyes—deep brown, nearly black—burned with such intensity that Dani felt the back of her knees wobble.

Somewhere along the chase, he had lost his jacket. His tie, too. His white dress shirt was damp with sweat, clinging to his chest and arms in a way that should've been illegal on international waters. The rolled-up sleeves exposed forearms that looked like they'd been designed by a very passionate Italian sculptor.

Her gaze dipped lower, despite her brain shouting for restraint.

Lean hips. Nice package. *I hope I didn't damage that too much.* Long legs—

Dani yanked her eyes back up to his face before her good sense slapped her.

Focus, Dani. Focus. You want to escape, not rip his clothes off.

"Listen," she began, holding up a hand in a placating gesture. "It looks like you're having a splendid party. Sorry for the punch. That was a gut reaction. I really do appreciate the rescue, but, well... I've gotta go."

Her voice was breathless, annoyingly so. She hated how weak she sounded when she was running on adrenaline, fear, and hunger.

For food, Dani, not him. Food!

To her surprise, the man didn't immediately leap for her or call for backup. Instead, he stopped, frowning as if she was the confusing part of this equation.

His eyes swept over her, lingering for one frustrating second too long on the way her dress had slid down to reveal one rounded lobe covered by a thin piece of black fabric. Of course, her body reacted to his intense stare. Her face flamed as her nipples hardened.

It's the cooler air, girl, not him. He wants to strangle you remember? The punch. You just reminded him of the low blow.

His eyes returned to her face, and he lifted an eyebrow, as if he knew what she was thinking.

"And where do you plan to go?" he asked, his voice cool, low, and disturbingly steady. "In case you haven't realized it, you've reached the end. There's nowhere else to go."

"That may stop other people," she said, one foot sliding closer to the railing. "It won't stop me."

Her hand slid behind her, feeling for the curved fiberglass housing of the lower lifeboat. If she could just hop onto it, she could dive without breaking her neck.

"You, uh... you've got a little fish egg... right here," she said, motioning vaguely to her cheekbone, trying to buy herself a few seconds of distraction.

He raised a hand and wiped at the spot she pointed to. He flicked the gooey remains of caviar onto the deck with a grimace.

"I hate the stuff," Dani added helpfully. "I have no idea why people eat it. It's like eating baitfish, only worse."

He didn't laugh.

I wonder if the Devil looks this yummy. If he does, I can see why people keep making poor decisions.

"Will you just shut up already?" she hissed, backing further along the railing. "I'm in enough trouble without you making it worse."

He blinked. "Who are you talking to?"

"My idiot side," she confessed, shooting him a wry smile. "We talk frequently… not that it helps."

His eyebrows shot up. "Are you… wired? Is that what all this drama is about? A story for tomorrow's tabloids?"

"Wired? Tabloids?" Dani gave him a bewildered frown. "No! I'm a mechanic. The only wiring I deal with is on engines."

"A mechanic? You expect me to believe you are a mechanic?" he repeated, incredulous, like she'd just claimed to be a dolphin trainer or a time traveler.

"Yes, a mechanic," she snapped, tugging the work boots tighter under her arm. "I fix engines. I was hired to fix this yacht's engine. Which, by the way, had nothing wrong with it except its sleazy owner."

"You mean Vito."

"*Ding-ding-ding*, we have a winner!" she replied, giving him a sarcastic thumbs up.

The man's jaw ticked. "And your name is—?"

"Not relevant right now," she said, gritting her teeth. "Tell Vito I want my tool bag back. And he's getting a whopper of a bill. I charge by the hour."

"I bet you do," the man retorted, his voice dipping into dangerous territory. "How much?"

Her brow furrowed in confusion. "How much for what?"

"How much do you charge per hour?"

"Two twenty-five," she said without hesitation, doubling her normal price.

His eyebrows lifted slightly. "I'll triple it."

Her lips parted in surprise. "Triple what—?"

"Hell, I'll pay you a flat fee. One hundred thousand."

Her mouth opened. Closed. Opened again.

"One hundred—?"

"Okay, five hundred."

That did it. The fog in her brain thickened, descended like a San Francisco summer. She shook her head like a dog coming out of water. "Five hundred thousand? What are you—what are we talking about right now?"

"You," he said, taking another step toward her. "One night. And me. Five hundred thousand."

Dani stared at him like he'd grown an extra head, possibly a golden one.

"I—what? No. No. I'm not—*no way!*" she stammered, scrambling sideways along the railing, her boots thumping against her ribs. "This isn't that kind of party. I don't do that. I'm just—"

His gaze dropped to her mouth, before moving lower. She backed away faster.

"You're insane. You know that, right?"

He gave a half-shrug, as if that was a perfectly acceptable accusation.

Dani stared at the man as if he had just proposed they duel with chainsaws at dawn.

"Five hundred thousand dollars," he repeated, his voice low, steady, and absurdly confident. "One night. You and me. Or do you want more?"

She blinked.

Once.

Twice.

Her brain, reeling from his absurd proposal, finally caught up and translated the fire in his eyes—it wasn't fury, not even righteous male ego—it was something far more dangerous.

Heat.

Desire. Full, primal, rip-her-clothes-off-on-the-deck desire.

It hit her like a rogue wave. A wild rush of heat flushed through her core, stealing the breath right from her lungs.

And if there was going to be death, it would be from pleasure. She was sure of that now. Sweet, delicious pleasure that would leave her melted like chocolate in the sun.

Or his eyes. Yeah, definitely his eyes.

"Oh no. Oh no! I'm not... You think that... I'm still a... Okay, I'm going now," she choked out, panic and hormones doing battle in her throat.

Without waiting for a response, Dani spun and scrambled up onto the fiberglass housing. Her hand fumbled for the hem of her slipping gown. With one hand clutching her dress and the other gripping her work boots...

This is it. One heartbeat, one leap. Maybe I'll wake up tomorrow bruised but free—

She tried not to think about the fact that she might not wake up at all. Taking a deep breath, she launched herself into the night before she could change her mind.

For a split second, she wondered if she'd misjudged the height—because the fall seemed to stretch into eternity.

Seconds later, the lukewarm waters of the Mediterranean swallowed her whole.

The impact felt like an open-handed slap, threatening to steal the breath she had hastily gulped. A momentary sense of disorientation wrapped around her before she kicked—hard, feeling the chill of the water seep into her skin. Breaking the surface, she gasped and dragged the gown over her head. Flipping onto her back, she wadded the fabric into a clumsy bundle, threading her bootlaces on either side of the material before she tied the thin material firmly around her waist. If she was lucky, the knot would hold until she reached the docks. If not, she would be adding a new pair of work boots to Vito's bill. In less than a minute, she was doing an awkward crawl toward the lights of the dock in the distance.

Her muscles screamed in protest, but a sense of exhilaration filled her, lifting her spirits. She had done it! A triumphant laugh escaped her lips; she had done it, against all odds! She had officially pulled off her insane escape!

Now, to reach the dock.

Her spirit was buoyed until she heard loud shouts, followed by a splash echoing behind her.

Dani twisted in the water, her legs pumping to keep her afloat. The familiar theme song from every shark movie ever made started playing in her head. Her heart skipped a beat.

A sudden splash nearby made her whirl around, her heart pounding in her chest. Releasing a breath, she recoiled as a deep, furious male voice shattered the darkness just a few feet from her.

"What the hell do you think you're doing? Have you lost your mind?" the man demanded, sputtering as he swam up beside her.

"You jumped in after me? Are you crazy?!" she shouted back, half-choking on seawater as she sank beneath the surface in surprise. She kicked upward and spat out a mouthful of saltwater. "Go back to the boat!"

"I should ask you the same thing, but I already know the answer!"

She turned and swam harder, fueled now by equal parts rage and disbelief. Her tied gown was weighing her down, and her boots felt like twin water anchors.

"Go away!" she barked over her shoulder.

"Why did you jump off the yacht?" he called out.

She twisted her head just enough to glare at him. "Maybe because I don't like being kidnapped and locked up!"

His stroke faltered. "Kidnapped? Who the hell kidnapped you?"

"Vito Marino—after he dumped a bottle of champagne on me and tricked me into believing it was all a mistake!"

"What were you even doing on the yacht in the first place?"

Dani huffed, rolling onto her back. She fumbled, pulling her boots up and draining them so she could rest them on her stomach. She might have to ditch them. They weren't worth drowning over. Neither was the gown. Her arms were starting to ache, and her body was so done with today.

"I told you—I'm a mechanic. I fix engines. I was hired to check the yacht's system. Only it turned out there wasn't anything wrong with them. Vito just wanted to meet the 'pretty girl with the wrench' he saw working on another boat. So congratulations, your buddy is a creep and a liar."

The man swore—loudly and in Greek.

The string of words was so colorful, Dani barked a laugh mid-kick.

"Sounds like you're not exactly Team Vito either."

He grunted. "Considering that is *my* yacht... no, I'm not."

Dani stopped swimming, letting herself float in the waves like a piece of driftwood. She twisted to stare at him in the dark, wide-eyed.

"Your yacht?!"

Before he could answer, a beam of light swept across the water from the right. She turned toward it, shielding her eyes against the spotlight as the soft purr of a motor approached.

"Over here!" the man called, lifting his arm.

Seconds later, a sleek black Zodiac skimmed up beside them. A crewman leaned over the edge, arm outstretched.

"I've got her, sir."

"Hey—wait a minute!" Dani squeaked, twisting when firm hands wrapped around her waist and lifted her clean out of the water like she weighed nothing more than a sodden beach towel.

"I don't need getting! I was going to the docks!" she snapped, wriggling.

"You'll thank us when the sharks show up," the man muttered.

Before she could properly argue, the man she'd punched hoisted himself up and swung over the side in one fluid motion. Water streamed from his soaked shirt down his forearms, while his trousers were molded to his frame. Dani hated how distracting that was.

She scowled, dripping and furious, but secretly a little impressed.

"Nice chase, by the way," she muttered, tiredly sitting back to rest against the side of the boat.

He glanced at her, dark eyes narrowing. "Nice punch."

"Touché," she retorted with a cheeky grin.

CHAPTER 2

The wind cut sharp and chilly across the open water, drying the salt against his skin and slicing through his soaked clothing, but Alexandros barely noticed. His attention was fixed on the woman beside him—the one who had punched him in the groin, hurled caviar at his face, and leapt off a mega-yacht to escape him.

She sat huddled like a shipwrecked goddess, tangled in a crimson gown that she had somehow tied around her waist during her exploits.

He should *loathe* how intrigued he was by her.

He should *question* her sanity, yet he couldn't help but admire her guts, her creativity, and her humor.

He should be *fighting the urge* to touch her again under the guise of practicality. Instead, he wanted to wrap himself around her. Or better yet, feel her wrapped around him.

He'd had models, heiresses, and movie stars clinging to his arm like designer handbags. But none of them had ever looked at him the way she did—like she was trying to decide whether to throw him overboard or use him for fish bait.

His gaze flicked to her sodden boots. She had miraculously not lost them during her dangerous and daring escape. They were still tied around her waist with the stubborn loyalty of a sailor clinging to her tools.

She looked half-drowned, half-feral, and completely out of place among the ultra-polished members of his world.

His desire for her was a primal urge, a physical ache that overshadowed all logical thought, a raw, visceral need. He saw her almost like a beautiful mermaid, her mysterious allure captivating him with every graceful movement and enigmatic smile. She was wild, elusive, and determined to escape him. In a world of materialistic women, she stood out—a unique and precious gem, untouched and undiscovered, sparkling with a purity that was both captivating and unexpected.

Although she didn't fit the classical mold of beauty, there was a raw, captivating energy about her that was undeniably attractive. Her beauty wasn't the kind that wilted under close examination; instead, it intensified, revealing hidden depths and captivating details like a fine painting.

Her round face was soft and full, with a gentle curve to her cheeks. Her startlingly green eyes, a little too big, held an expression of innocent curiosity. Her tiny, exquisitely formed nose was pert, delicate, and perfect for her face. Her nostrils were flaring slightly, as if she was debating returning to the water—or worse, attacking him again.

She looked more like a drowned pixie than a person. Her body was compact, not petite. She had a toned physique, suggesting regular exercise, but lacked the sharp muscle definition typical of weightlifters.

She was a natural beauty—one who didn't need diamonds, designer dresses, or makeup to turn heads.

No, he thought, letting his gaze drift over the black sports bra clinging to her skin. *She is a wildcat, fierce and untamed, with a mouth that could cut steel, and she packs a powerful punch—literally.*

To his astonishment, he realized that she was probably exactly what she claimed to be.

A mechanic.

And something far more dangerous—unapologetically herself.

Alexandros turned to Demetrius, his head of security, who sat stone-faced at the console like a statue carved out of wind and duty.

"Have a car waiting at the dock," he said over the engine hum. "And have warm and dry clothing delivered from the yacht for my guest and myself."

"Nothing for me—thanks. I won't be hanging around once we get to shore," she said.

"Do you plan on leaving in your undergarments?" he bit back.

She shrugged her slender shoulders and pulled her legs up as far as she could while retaining her death grip on her boots. He shook his head and muttered a low curse.

Demetrius's lips twitched, but he gave a curt nod and tapped his earpiece.

Alexandros turned back to the woman beside him. Her fingers were pale and trembling despite the warm weather. Her hair was a mass of wet curls that stuck to her forehead, her jaw, her neck. He wasn't sure if her hair was black or brown. The temptation to reach out and rub it between his fingers made him grit his teeth.

The night air hit cold and sharp against his soaked skin, a jarring contrast to the molten heat still coiling low in his stomach.

Mikrouli mou, he thought, the endearment rising unbidden. *What the hell just happened? What is it about her?* he groused, his temper simmering like a bed of hot coals.

He sighed when she shivered again.

He glanced down at his own arms, wet and useless. Harold—one of the younger security crew—held out a thick towel.

Alexandros took the plush towel without a word and turned back to her. He hesitated for a fraction of a second. She could bite, he was sure of it—but he couldn't leave her shivering.

She was watching him through her lashes, warily, like a cat ready to scratch.

He didn't speak. He just lifted the towel and motioned for her to lean forward.

Her lips parted as if she was about to argue. She glared at him, but surprised him when she released an exhausted sigh and relented. She leaned closer, cautious but not flinching.

Good. He wasn't sure he could handle it if she flinched.

He wrapped the towel around her shoulders, tucking it around her with far more care than he'd used on a living human being in years. It gave him an excuse to draw her closer. She hesitated, her body rigid. He sensed that she didn't give her trust easily.

The warmth of the towel and his body was enough to lure her for a second, just a second, into feeling safe. He liked that. He liked that a lot. Resting his chin against the top of her head, he breathed in her scent—the faintest trace of jasmine from her shampoo and salt from the water. The combination of her body pressed against his and her scent hit him harder than he'd expected.

His arms tightened protectively around her when she continued to tremble. Exhaustion, cold, and probably shock layered thick around her, but she still clutched those boots like armor.

He couldn't help it—he smiled.

Not a smirk. A real, honest smile. When was the last time that had happened? Hell, when was the last time he cared whether he had smiled?

"What's your name?" he asked quietly.

She let out a soft breath, her lips slightly blue. "I would tell you it was Helga, but Vito already blasted it to everyone on board. It's Dani."

"Dani," he repeated, tasting the sound of it. "Short for Danielle?"

She shrugged against him. "Just Dani."

No explanation. No attempt at charm. No flirtation. Just a shrug. Like his name, his yacht, his perfectly tailored world didn't impress her in the slightest.

"I'm Alexandros," he offered. "Alexandros Kallistratos."

She blinked up at him. "Uh-huh."

That was it. No wide eyes. No breathy repetition of his name. Just another shrug, like she'd met ten billionaires before breakfast and didn't have time to be dazzled today.

The Zodiac slowed as it approached the dock, the gentle lapping of waves breaking the quiet. Alexandros realized he hadn't been breathing properly since he had pulled himself out of the water. It had nothing to do with his chase or swim. He suspected it had everything to do with the woman in his arms. Every moment with her had been sharpened to a knife-edge, he realized. And he didn't want it to end.

Harold jumped out, landing lightly on the dock, and moved to tie off the bowline and stern. His onshore security team moved with their usual precision—efficient, silent—but Alexandros barely noticed. His world had shifted, and all of it now centered on one dripping, defiant woman.

But, Dani noticed. His lips curved into a grin when she muttered under her breath, '*It's like living in a glass jar*', and rolled her eyes.

She uncoiled slowly, untying the gown from around her waist and holding it out to him like a dead jellyfish. He took it without a word as he tried to shield her body from his security detail. She ignored him and everyone else, tugging the towel from around her shoulders.

"Turn around," he ordered harshly in Greek, scowling at the men who quickly followed his order.

"It's a little late for modesty. Besides, my underwear cover more than most of the dresses at that fancy party you're throwing," she drawled as she wrapped the damp towel around her waist and secured it with a firm tuck. "See, all better."

It wasn't. Her nipples strained against her top, hard pebbles that made him grit his teeth. He unfastened his dress shirt and yanked it off. She started when she realized what he was doing. She was even more startled when he took her boots from her and slid her arms into his shirt before buttoning it up.

"You'll be cold," she muttered, her voice husky.

He swallowed a low groan when she ran a slender finger down his sternum. His jaw clenched when she wound a finger in his chest hair and tugged it.

"Yep, you've got goosebumps," she teased, her finger trailing lightly down his chest. "Even your nipples are hard."

Self-combustion. That's what is about to happen to me, he thought, his gaze locking with her teasing ones.

He stroked her cheek. "You are playing with fire, *mikroula mou*," he warned.

"Just making sure you didn't suffer any injuries from your adventure," she teased.

He swallowed when she bent, her head moving down as if to—

He groaned at his wayward thoughts and watched with glittering eyes as she picked up her boots. Her waterlogged footwear landed with a thud on the dock before she used Demetrius's turned shoulder as support and climbed out of the boat ahead of him.

Before he could follow, she spun to face him, planting her feet like she was defending sacred ground. The towel slipped a little, so she cinched it again around her waist. Her cheeks heated when he followed her movements. She shot him her best, fierce expression.

"You stay," she ordered, lifting her hand to stop him. "This part of the rescue ends here. I appreciate the shoulder, and the shirt, but as the saying goes, all good things must end. And darlin', this thrilling little adventure is definitely over."

She flashed him an amused grin. He had no doubt that she knew perfectly well the effect she was having on him—and enjoyed every second of the torture she was inflicting. His mermaid was warning him to stay away.

That will never happen, he vowed, returning her gaze with a promise of his own reflected in his.

He loved the way she swallowed and lifted her chin. His challenge was being accepted whether she realized it or not.

"You can give Vito back the dress. Remind him that my tool bag is to be returned with all tools present and accounted for, or he will truly regret his actions. I'll be sending him an invoice. I suggest he pay it if he doesn't want me dismantling every engine he owns."

"Message received. Now, may I disembark?" he dryly requested.

She shook her head and pointed outward. "Vito's that way—and so are my tools."

He arched a brow. "You're refusing to allow me to exit my boat?"

"Yes—because you've got a message to deliver. Once that's done, what you do is none of my business," she said.

"Ah, yes, I remember. The threatening message—for Vito. Got it," he replied, his lips twitching at her audacity.

"Yeah. Plus, I don't trust you."

His brow furrowed. "For heaven's sake, why not? I just risked my life trying to save you!"

"First, I didn't ask for you to save me. I could have swum here without you slowing me down. Second, you offended me. I don't like guys who offend me."

"And how did I offend you?" he asked, crossing his arms.

"By assuming I could be bought. Honestly, you couldn't afford me. I'm worth a hell of a lot more than five hundred measly thousand, trust me," she retorted.

"You're right, that was offensive," he reluctantly admitted.

"Damn right it was."

"I want to see you again," he stated.

Dani snorted out an amused laugh and shook her head. "No, but you can do me a favor."

"Anything."

She stepped closer to the edge of the dock, bending until they were less than a foot apart. If he reached up, he could wrap his arms around her waist, pull her back down into the zodiac, and order Demetrius to return them to the yacht where he could make love to her all night long.

Damn, but she has the most incredible eyes.

He was momentarily distracted. Something that he was not used to. He blinked when she snapped her fingers in front of his face.

"Ah, yes. The favor. What do you wish?" he responded, a teasing smile curving his lips.

"I wish, Genie, for you to get me my tool bag—and yourself better friends. The ones you have suck," she murmured before she straightened and turned away.

Alexandros blinked and watched as Dani strode across the dock to a motorbike parked at the entrance. It didn't matter that she was barefoot and dripping. She still radiated heat and defiance like a flame that wouldn't go out—all while wearing her undergarments, his shirt, and a towel. He released a long, slow breath and shook his head in wonder.

"Follow her, and make sure she makes it back to her home safely," he instructed.

"I'll do it myself," Demetrius responded with a low chuckle. "That one, she is trouble."

Alexandros chuckled. "Yes. Yes, she is. And she is going to be my trouble. I want a full report on her. I want to know everything about her."

A strange fire had ignited inside him—one that could challenge the fires of Hades.

He'd never met anyone like her.

And now?

He couldn't imagine wanting anyone else.

DANI TRIED NOT to think about the infuriatingly handsome billionaire who had jumped off his perfectly good yacht after her.

"Better than a perfectly good plane," she mused.

If she hadn't been so upset about her missing tool bag, she might have gone a little easier on him—

"Or not," she ruefully conceded.

She grimaced as she reached down the front of her boy-short undies and extracted her cell phone and scooter key. She held both up like a magician revealing her ultimate trick. The key to her Vespa was blessedly dry and her phone only slightly damp—thanks to a creative mix of double-layered shower caps and a full roll of first aid tape she'd found under the vanity in the room Vito had locked her in.

MacGyver would've been proud.

She untied her boot strings, dropping them to the smooth, synthetic boards under her feet. Hopping, she slid one on before stepping into the other. A grimace of distaste twisted her expression at the squishy interior.

"My toes are going to rival Grandpa's—minus the hair—" she sighed, visualizing her shriveled digits with distaste.

She was anything but elegant stomping along the narrow path back to the warehouse where she had left her motorbike. Her boots thudded with each step as she walked.

She knew she looked a mess—and couldn't care less. The towel made an adequate skirt, Alexandros' shirt was tied over it to make the towel more secure, her sports bra looked like one of the midriff tops that were popular, and her boots could be a new fashion trend. The dock was illuminated under the overhead lights and the moonlight. Shadows stretched long and quiet around her as the rhythmic lap of the waves created the familiar lullaby of the sea.

Her Vespa sat just where she left it—perched at the far end of the dock, sleek and cherry red like a candy-coated promise of freedom. The *Elettrica 70* decal gleamed under the dock lamps, and the seat still had the towel she used to protect it from the sun.

She used her key to unlock the side basket, and pulled out her helmet. She tucked her wayward tangle of hair under the helmet as best she could before she straddled the scooter with a sigh. She didn't start the engine just yet. Instead, she sat, breathing in the salt-kissed air and letting the breeze cool her damp skin.

God, she was tired.

And rattled.

She looked out at the brightly lit yacht. Faint music and laughter could be heard. If nothing else, she had given them something to talk about tonight.

She pursed her lips when the annoying image of Alexandros Kallistratos popped into her head. His irritating, confident smirk kept flickering in her mind like a stubborn flame. Not the part where she'd punched him. Not even the part where he offered her half a million like she was a sequined call girl. No—it was that moment in the water. When their gazes had locked. When her pulse had jumped for a reason that had nothing to do with danger.

Nope. Nope, nope, nope.

She was putting all thoughts of him straight into the deep freeze.

She knew men like him. Gorgeous, rich, and carved from stone, with enough power to buy anything they wanted—and none of it was permanent. Guys like him weren't looking for girlfriends or wives. They wanted affairs, flings, something exciting and forgettable. They made you feel like a goddess until the next shiny distraction came along.

If she'd wanted a fling, she had options. She could have her pick from the dozens of charming deckhands, cocky fishermen, and overly friendly restaurateurs who offered her free calamari and discount espresso on the regular. Or she could make the mistake of trusting a liar's smooth charm. She had done that once—and she had paid the price. It had cost her, her dignity—and nearly her life.

She wasn't interested in becoming someone's salty summer memory. She wanted more. Something real—like her parents had.

With someone I can trust.

She glanced toward the water again, watching the glint of lights reflecting on the dark Mediterranean. Five years she'd been at this—working her way from island to island, learning everything she could about boats, engines, and surviving on her own terms. She'd seen every kind of man walk into her life… and right back out again.

All except one.

Her phone lit up with a call, and a snort of laughter slipped from her lips as she reached for the mic control on her helmet. The contact read: Grumpsicle.

"Speak of the devil," she teased, answering with a grin. "Did you feel a disturbance in the Force or something?"

"Danika Rae Collins," came the gravelly voice on the other end. "Why do I feel you're in trouble?"

She laughed outright, pushed the motorbike off its stand, cranked the throttle, and rolled away from the dock. The electric scooter purred beneath her, smooth and familiar.

"Define 'trouble'. If it involves sequins, an unexpected nighttime swim, and a yacht owned by an overconfident Greek demigod, then maybe."

"Oh, Lord." He groaned. "Do I even want to know?"

"I'll tell you everything. Just as soon as I get home and cleaned up. You're going to love this one, Grandpa. It starts with champagne and ends with caviar combat."

His deep chuckle rumbled through the line. "How about you tell me about it now? And you better not exaggerate."

"I won't. But I'm pretty sure I broke the space-time continuum of awkward encounters tonight."

She turned onto the coastal road, the wind whipping at the damp ends of her hair as she rode. Her headlights carved a steady beam through the night, highlighting narrow turns and the occasional feral cat darting across the road.

Behind her, at a cautious distance, a sleek black SUV followed. Silent. Steady.

Dani didn't see it yet. She was so enthralled with the tale that her grandfather had refused to wait to hear about.

She was also too busy laughing at her own ridiculous night.

"You did what? Just thinking about that makes me cringe, girl," Stuart replied.

"I popped a home run, right into his groin. Of course, I thought it was Vito," she repeated.

"Oh, lordy, girl. What am I going to do with you?" Stuart groaned.

"Love me like you always do, Gramps," she replied, her voice softening.

"Be careful, love. I don't want to have to come bury any bodies— but you know I would if he broke your heart," Stuart warned.

She swallowed, slowing as she turned into the marina on the other side of the cove, where she lived and worked. She drew to a stop along where the trawler she and her grandfather had refurbished was docked. She looked out across the bay, but she couldn't see the yacht from this angle. There were too many other pleasure crafts blocking the view.

"I will, Gramps. I'm thinking it might be time to move on again."

"Listen to your gut and do what you think is right. If you need me to come out there, just ask—or... maybe it's time for you to come home," he said.

Her head was already shaking before he finished. Tears burned her eyes. Even after all these years, she still wasn't ready.

"Soon, Gramps, but… not yet." She breathed out, feeling her fatigue pulling at her. "I'll call you tomorrow. I'm bushed."

"Love you, darling. I'm here whenever you need me."

"I know. I love you, too, Gramps. Good night," she murmured.

Dani sighed and slid off her motorbike. She replaced the helmet in the side basket and secured the chain and lock attached to the piling, so her only mode of transportation couldn't be stolen.

She locked the trawler's salon doors behind her with a satisfying click. The ridiculous red dress had been tossed somewhere in her brain's mental recycling bin, right between 'awkward sea rescues' and 'idiotic billionaires'.

Nope. No more billionaires, she silently promised herself. *Especially not the Greek god kind with eyes that made you forget your own name. Nope. Not happening. Not tomorrow. Never,* she vowed, heading for the shower.

Outside, Demetrius stood in the shadows, watching the unusual woman he had fished out of the water disappear into a 1950s trawler. The vibration of his phone made him smile. He reached up and touched his earpiece to connect.

"She is safe," he answered in greeting.

"You have her address?"

"She lives on a trawler at Pier 5."

"Is she alone?"

Demetrius's smile grew. "I can't be certain, but I believe she is alone. I'll have more information for you by tomorrow."

"Good. Post a team to make sure she remains safe," Alexandros ordered.

"Yes, sir."

Demetrius chuckled under his breath as the call ended. He had watched over Alexandros since he was a boy. Over the last ten years, he had grown more concerned about Alexandros' growing cynicism. All of that may have changed tonight as a defiant young woman pointed out something to the man he thought of as a son—that Alexandros needed better friends.

"Finally!"

Demetrius shook his head, grinning. Dani had no idea that her story with Alexandros was far from over.

Or that the man she was trying so hard to ignore had just made her his next priority.

CHAPTER 3

The sun was barely over the horizon the next morning when Dani navigated the narrow road into the boatyard. The gravel road curved along the shore like a lazy serpent, hugging the slope of the bay before flattening out into cracked pavement peppered with oil stains, tire grooves, and a smattering of crushed beer cans. The boatyard always smelled faintly of diesel, fish, sun-baked metal, and fresh saltwater—and Dani wouldn't have it any other way.

Her Vespa hummed like the wings of a hummingbird as she eased off the throttle and rolled under the weather-worn sign that arched across the entrance: Kostas & Sons Marine Service. The paint had peeled long ago, leaving only faded blue letters and a sun-bleached dolphin logo that someone had once attempted to repaint with what looked like nail polish.

Morning light cut sharply through the slats of the boathouse roof. It danced off rows of hulls in varying states of repair and reflected off stainless steel, chrome, and fiberglass like sequins on that red dress she had worn the night before. Welders sparked to life on one side, an air compressor rumbled somewhere deeper in, and the occasional clang of tools echoed between the corrugated metal walls.

"Hey Dani!"

"Mornin', Dani!"

"Got time to tune my girl up later?"

A chorus of familiar voices rose in greeting as she cruised past rows of fishing boats and luxury weekend cruisers. Every guy with a wrench seemed to find a reason to straighten up and grin as she passed, their faces hopeful, eager, or just plain amused.

She lifted one hand in a lazy wave, her towel-now-skirt from last night long gone, replaced by her go-to uniform of grease-stained cargo pants, a black tank top, and a stubborn ponytail barely contained beneath her helmet.

They were good guys.

Mostly harmless.

And definitely not her type.

She turned toward the side warehouse, its tall sliding doors already cracked open to let in the breeze, and coasted the scooter into the shadow of the overhang. The air shifted instantly—cooler, quieter, a haven of steel, sweat, and forgotten tales from the sea.

She was just swinging off the seat when two brawny arms caught her around the waist and lifted her clean off the ground.

"Gotcha!"

"Carlos!" she yelped, half-laughing, half-scowling. "Put me down before I jam a spark plug into your ear!"

He spun her with practiced ease and set her down, only to lean in and plant a loud, obnoxious kiss on her cheek when she turned her head at the last second. She playfully punched him in the stomach—hard enough to make him grunt.

"One of these days, I am going to deck you," she warned, brushing him off with mock irritation. "You've been asking for it since Tunisia."

Carlos grinned, utterly unrepentant, his teeth white against sun-darkened skin. "You'd miss me."

"Like I'd miss food poisoning," she muttered, tugging open the scooter's storage bin and exchanging her helmet for her backup tool bag with a grunt.

"How's Maria?" she asked, feigning innocence even as she braced herself.

Carlos's grin faltered. "Gone," he said dramatically, holding a hand over his heart. "Left me for a pastry chef in Santorini. Can you believe that? A man who bakes! I never stood a chance."

Dani groaned. "Carlos…"

"Don't feel bad for me," he said, brightening like the human embodiment of a bad idea. "Now that I'm single again, you can finally admit you're in love with me."

"Not in this lifetime, *mi amigo*." She shoved him backward with a foot.

He cackled and danced away, dodging her second kick. "So, what's on the docket today, *mi sirena mecánica*?"

"Rebuilding the heads on those twin inboards from the Mistral," she replied, slinging the bag over her shoulder and jerking her chin toward the ladder leading into a weather-beaten fishing trawler elevated on supports.

"Fancy. I've got a few outboards from that rental place in the next bay." He glanced at her sideways. "How'd the job go yesterday? The mega yacht—you know, the one everyone is talking about? Was it everything you imagined and more?"

Dani's fingers curled tighter around the handle of her bag. "It was a job," she said flatly, already climbing the ladder.

Carlos watched her go, brow furrowed, before he shrugged. "I'll check on you later. Try not to electrocute yourself or fall in love with someone else without telling me, okay?"

"Please go beg Maria for forgiveness so I don't have to babysit you," Dani shot back over her shoulder.

"You wound me," Carlos called out, hand over his heart again. "But I still love you. I know you will one day love me back!"

She rolled her eyes, lifted her hand, and waved him off without turning around. His laughter followed her up the ladder.

Dani dropped her bag with a thunk next to the engine compartment and pulled the tarp off the engines. Her hands were already moving on autopilot—checking, unscrewing, inspecting while her mind wandered.

The physical work soothed her. Or at least, it normally did.

But no matter how deeply she buried herself in carburetors and timing chains, Alexandros Kallistratos's face kept drifting into view. Those maddening dark eyes. The way his voice had curled around her name like smoke. The absurd, inconvenient, undeniable way her body had reacted when he touched her.

What the hell was wrong with her?

It had been almost four years since she'd felt even a flicker of interest in someone—and the last time had been a disaster. If her grandfather hadn't been there to talk reason into her head, if she hadn't finally listened—really listened—to the warning in her gut, things could have turned out much, much different.

She pressed her hand to her chest as the memory rose—uninvited, unwanted, and all too clear.

She swallowed and braced her palms against the cool metal of the engine, staring down into the shadows of the bilge.

Her breathing slowed. Her fingers tightened. The scent of sea air and oil twisted, transforming into the thick, spiced breeze of another coast.

She closed her eyes, and the familiar memories of regret pulled her back to another place, another time…

∾

FOUR YEARS EARLIER:

DANI STROLLED along the cobbled streets as dusk settled in Tangier. She loved everything about it. It was where the Mediterranean kissed the edge of Africa and the streets blazed with color and life.

The call to prayer was ringing out from the mosques, echoing over the terracotta rooftops as the city transformed into something golden and ancient—something out of a storybook.

She breathed in a deep, calming breath. At seventeen, she still felt raw, but this magical place had swept away most of the nightmares she still had whenever she closed her eyes.

She loved the cobbled alleys scented with mint tea and orange blossoms, the golden light brushing the shoulders of passersby, the way laughter and music floated like petals through the narrow streets.

And she loved Zayan Alaoui.

A thrill ran through her, and she wrapped her arms around her waist to hug herself. She had stumbled into Zayan almost a month ago in the market when she was purchasing some fruits and vegetables for herself and her grandfather.

He had appeared in the Grand Socco like some desert prince in a half-buttoned shirt and linen trousers. Her smile softened when she thought of the half-crooked grin he always had on his lips. His eyes were the color of fresh coffee and just as addictive. He spoke five languages, all of them like poetry.

One look and her heart leapt as if it recognized him.

One touch made her forget how to breathe.

"You are so beautiful, my Dani. More beautiful than the waters, the stars, the very heavens above."

Even now, as she hurried to surprise him, she could feel excitement building inside her. He made her want to laugh again. He made her soul dance.

She'd pushed away her grandfather's gentle warning when he caught her slipping off their trawler shortly after lunch. Yet, she couldn't erase what he said from her mind.

"Dani, there are men in this world who only want one thing from a beautiful girl like you. They'll whisper sweet nothings and make promises they have no intention of keeping. It's the thrill of the hunt for them. The challenge is to see who they can conquer. They don't think of the broken hearts they leave behind."

"Zayan's not like that! He loves me. He makes me feel... special, Gramps."

Stuart sighed. "What does your gut tell you, love?"

"It tells me—it tells me— I... don't know. I want to believe—"

God, she needed to believe someone could see her—really see her —beyond the grief still clinging to her like ash.

She thought of the first night she had met up with Zayan. The memories caused little butterflies to flutter in her stomach. The night had been magical. The moonlight had painted the city in silver. Under the cover of night, she had slipped away from the trawler to meet with him. They had laughed and explored the labyrinth of lantern-lit stalls, the air thick with the smells of exotic spices and roasting meats, and hidden rooftop cafes, their music spilling out onto the streets. Beneath a sky scattered with a million glittering stars, he'd played a haunting melody on his oud, whispering her name as if it held the weight of the universe.

And when he kissed her...

For a moment, she forgot the sound of metal twisting. Forgot the blood. The screams. The way her mother's hand had slipped from hers, going cold.

In Zayan's arms, she'd felt the carefree innocence of her youth return, a lightness she'd almost forgotten. Whole. Seen.

Within days, he had proposed a whirlwind escape—the scent of paella in Spain, the sound of bouzouki music in Greece, and a life together in countless breathtaking places. With a fervent hope in his eyes, he'd promised freedom, a life unburdened by chains. Passion. A life of adventure.

She had laughed and said no. But, Zayan's daily requests to elope, to experience the passion he felt for her, had been relentless, leaving her feeling both intrigued and overwhelmed. She'd refused his desire for intimacy, but the battle was slipping from her grasp as a quiet desperation settled in her heart. Every time he kissed her, a fiery longing consumed her, leaving her breathless and wanting more.

Dani wrapped her arms around her waist as she walked. She couldn't forget the look in her grandfather's warm brown eyes. There had been compassion, understanding, and... grief. She realized that she wasn't the only one hurting. She lifted a hand to wipe the tear that coursed down her cheek.

Am I making a mistake? Will I regret this for the rest of my life if I tell him no?

She drew a shuddering breath and looked both ways before she crossed the busy street. She was heading to find Zayan earlier than their arranged time. They usually met in the early evenings. She had to tell him that their love would need to wait. That she... wasn't ready —not yet.

Her spiraling thoughts shattered into disbelief the moment she rounded the corner. Pain swept through her when she almost bumped into the couple who were locked in a passionate embrace.

Zayan—the man-boy who swore he loved her—was wrapped around a girl in a white dress. He was holding a suitcase in one hand.

He wasn't just kissing the girl, he was repeating words he had spoken to *her*.

Dani listened, her heart silently breaking, as he whispered words of love, sharing promises of grand adventures together. Familiar words that she could have repeated almost verbatim.

Her breath shuddered when his hand curled around the girl's waist, and she watched with growing anger as he laughed and called the girl *azizi*—his darling.

All of it had been rehearsed. Practiced, she realized with growing disillusion.

Dani backed away, slipping back along the street she had just emerged from. She pressed her fist to her mouth. She wouldn't cry.

Instead, she followed Zayan—learning, and growing wiser. By early evening, she had watched him woo a girl from Sweden, another from Canada, and two boys, one from Germany and the other from France. All tourists. All spellbound.

Each one, thinking he or she were the only one.

Later that night, she arrived a few minutes early and waited across from where she and Zayan normally met. She watched him with a critical eye. He paused in front of a window. Her nose wiggled with disdain when he sprayed mouth freshener into his mouth and ran a comb through his black hair.

Her eyes narrowed when another handsome young man walked up to him. It was obvious what they were talking about from the way they were laughing.

Probably comparing notes.

Her lips curved into a satisfied smile as she watched three young women and a man stroll into the bustling plaza, the scent of spiced coffee and exotic food filling the air. Their expressions—furrowed brows and knowing glances—showed they'd compared notes. She watched, her breath catching in her throat as the color drained from Zayan's face, his usual smooth confidence shattering like fragile glass to be replaced with growing anger and desperation.

The three women, while the male watched with anger, had backed Zayan up against the front of a restaurant. From the angry yells and the laughter from the patrons, the women were giving Zayan a piece of their mind.

She winced when his white shirt and pants were suddenly coated with blobs of red sauce.

Okay, more than a piece of their mind.

His frantic gaze swept the plaza. She lifted her chin when his furious dark eyes landed on her. She lifted her hand to her lips and blew him a kiss before she turned and walked away. *He* didn't deserve any of her headspace.

She walked slowly back to the trawler. Her grandfather was sitting on the deck, sharpening a fishing knife with slow, deliberate strokes. He didn't ask her questions when she climbed aboard.

"I'm ready to move on," she said, her voice low and raw.

Stuart looked up, his brows furrowing. "You sure?"

She nodded once. "Yeah. I've seen what I needed to see."

He didn't press, which she was grateful for. He simply set the knife down, rose to his feet, and wrapped her in a hug that told her he understood more than he let on.

That night, Dani sat alone in her bunk, clutching her mother's old scarf and trying not to cry.

What cracked her heart wasn't Zayan's betrayal. It was the shattering of something far more fragile:

Hope.

And the last part of her innocence — that life didn't have to be painful.

There weren't many men out there like her grandfather and father. She stared at the smiling image of her dad, his arms wrapped around her and her mom. That had been something else she had witnessed while she had been following Zayan.

Maybe she could love again. That someone might love her—not for what she could give, but for who she was beneath the scars. But, she would never give in easily again.

No, if I find a guy I like, really like again, he's going to have to work for it.

She had learned a brutal life lesson.

Most guys didn't want love.

They didn't want a connection.

They just wanted a conquest. A warm body. A thrill. Before they disappeared, taking the other person's heart like a trophy.

She would never trust a man's pretty words again.

DANI EXHALED SHARPLY and blinked back to the present, the scent of diesel snapping her out of the memory.

She swiped at the sweat on her brow and shook her head as if she could scatter the thoughts loose. She'd buried Morocco. Buried Zayan, and all the smooth-talking guys that came after. They were all just another Carlos. Nice, fun in moderation, and never to be taken seriously.

So why the hell had Alexandros Kallistratos of all people made her want to see if he was different? His generous offer for a night should tell her *exactly* what kind of guy he was! An older version of Zayan! Smooth, confident, and full of the same steaming crap she'd been sold before.

She gritted her teeth and returned to the engine. There was work to be done—and no space in her heart for pretty lies in expensive suits.

CHAPTER 4

*H*e woke with a smile on his lips.

It had been years—years—since Alexandros Kallis-tratos had felt this brand of anticipation humming in his veins before his feet even hit the floor. A slow, lazy ache stretched through his muscles, and the image of tousled curls and flashing green eyes danced at the edges of his memory like smoke.

Dani.

The name curled in his mind with the same enigmatic sensuality that had haunted his dreams all night. Dreams that had been… vivid, to say the least. One minute she was dripping wet and defiant on his yacht, clutching her boots like a lifeline. Next, she was laughing—naked except for grease-smeared cargo pants—wielding a wrench like a weapon and daring him to get closer.

And he had. In the dream, he had gotten much closer.

He chuckled under his breath as he stepped out onto the shaded upper deck where breakfast awaited. The Aegean morning breeze skimmed across his bare arms, warm and salty, tousling his still-damp hair as he took his seat at the table set beneath the linen awning. His steward, Haralambos, approached with practiced grace and set down his breakfast—poached eggs on grilled bread with ripe fruit and a glass of fresh orange juice.

He barely had time to unfold his napkin before Demetrius appeared, folder in hand and an amused smile twitching the corners of his mouth.

"Good morning, Alexandros," Demetrius greeted, his tone just this side of innocent. "Did you sleep well?"

Alexandros gave him a lazy, knowing glance and nodded to the steward. "Join me."

Demetrius sat as Haralambos brought a second setting. He ordered espresso and yogurt with honey, and they waited in companionable silence until the steward disappeared again, leaving only the whisper of the sea and the soft clink of silverware.

Alexandros leaned forward, his elbow resting on the table as he reached for the folder.

"Is this her?" he asked, already knowing the answer.

Demetrius nodded. "Initial file. Took some digging."

Alexandros opened the folder and blinked.

One page.

One. Single. Page.

And not even filled with double-spaced typing.

He lifted the sheet and turned it over as if a fuller dossier might be hiding on the back. But the reverse was blank, as stark as the amused glint in Demetrius's eyes.

He read aloud, voice low with disbelief.

"Danika Rae Collins. Age twenty-one. American. Lives aboard a trawler at Pier Five named... *The Gentle Breeze.*"

He dropped the page and leaned back in his chair, brows rising as he shot Demetrius a look of dry inquiry. "That's it?"

Demetrius offered a grateful nod to the steward who returned with his coffee. He chuckled at Alexandros disgruntled expression.

"That's it. I ran the usual searches. Social media, digital trail, records—nothing. She might as well be a ghost."

Alexandros exhaled a long, slow breath and stared down at his eggs as if they might offer insight. "Incredible," he murmured. "In this world of influencers and over-sharers… I find the one woman who's completely offline."

Demetrius took a sip of his espresso, savoring it with a sigh. "She has an email address linked to an engine repair site she's never updated. No Instagram. No Twitter. No Facebook. No TikTok. She's a unicorn."

"A unicorn who punches like a prizefighter and tosses caviar into billionaires' faces," Alexandros dryly commented, his lips quirking at the memory of her pointing out where she had hit him.

That earned him a choked laugh from Demetrius.

"She was magnificent," Alexandros continued, voice lower now. "Hair soaked, that dress hanging off her like it was floating—bare feet, clutching those ridiculous boots like they were diamonds." He paused, eyes narrowing with interest. "Despite that, she carried herself like a queen storming a palace."

Demetrius raised a brow. "She also stole your shirt."

"Technically, I gave it to her," Alexandros corrected, though his smile had gone wistful. "Not that she cared for my act of chivalry. Or showed even the faintest flicker of being impressed."

He swirled his orange juice, watching the pulp catch the morning light.

"She wanted nothing from me, Demetrius. She didn't want my money. Didn't care about my name. She just wanted her tools."

"Alexandros, as your friend, I think this is one you should leave well enough alone. As your head of security, I ask that you at least give me time to find out more about her if you won't."

"I appreciate your concern, my friend, but this is one that has me truly intrigued. Something that hasn't happened in a long, long time," he said, lifting his fork and spearing a piece of toast with egg on it. "I don't want her to escape."

Demetrius leaned back in his chair, studying his employer like one might study a volcano that had grumbled after years of silence.

"So what now?" he asked.

Alexandros smiled over his coffee cup, his eyes dark with amusement and something else—something deeper.

"Now," he said, "I do things the old-fashioned way. I'll start by returning her precious tool bag. I'm sure that should earn me some credit. By tonight, she will be eating out of my hand."

Demetrius groaned. "I'm not sure who I should be feeling sorrier for—you or the woman."

"Sorrier for—me? Why would I need your sympathy?"

"When she hands you your balls on a platter like she nearly did last night, I'll explain," Demetrius dryly replied.

Alexandros tilted his head back and laughed. "Since when has a woman ever turned me down?" He raised his hand when Demetrius started to point out the obvious. "Last night does not count. She was upset with Vito. Who, by the way, is no longer welcome at any of my properties," he added.

"His sister is not going to be pleased about that," Demetrius warned, his face bland of any emotion.

"Perhaps it's time for Allegra to find a new best friend," he said.

Demetrius lifted his eyes to the heavens and muttered a low, "Thank you, Zeus, for small favors."

That drew another rich, genuine laugh from Alexandros. One that echoed across the deck and over the sea.

THE GRAVEL CRUNCHED beneath the tires of the silver Bentley Continental GT, its polished chrome grille glinting like a snarl beneath the sun. Alexandros ignored the stares as he guided the luxury coupe around a rusted flatbed truck and parked just outside the boathouse.

Men looked up from their work, some shading their eyes with grease-streaked hands, others nudging each other with sighs of longing in Greek. He could almost hear the rumors starting to brew: What the hell is a Kallistratos doing here?

Alexandros was, in fact, dressed down—navy slacks, a tailored white linen shirt with the sleeves rolled to his elbows, and dark aviators that hid the wicked amusement glinting in his eyes. He'd traded his power suit for something far more dangerous—a charm offensive.

And he came bearing gifts.

He stepped out, gripping the weighty tool bag in his right hand. The one she had left behind. Sacrificed like a lamb on his yacht during her escape.

Vito reluctantly confessed last night that he'd hidden the well-loved bag behind the bar in the brightly lit salon. The pudgy Italian had been pale and extremely apologetic by the time Alexandros had finished with him and had him escorted ashore.

He reached up and removed his sunglasses as he stepped into the service bay. The scent hit him first: sea salt, hot metal, oil, and a faint undertone of fish. He curled his nose. A place like this would send his private chef into early retirement.

A curious sound floated through the air—music, but not the kind he expected. Somewhere between Ludovico Einaudi and Enya. It wafted from the trawler propped up ahead on blocks like a patient in dry dock, her hull chipped and sun-faded.

He followed the sound.

A metallic clang, a muttered curse, and the unmistakable growl of someone losing an argument with an engine. A voice that sounded an awful lot like it came from his mermaid.

He stepped closer, and there she was.

Danika.

Her name rolled over his tongue like a caress. She would never be just Dani to him. She was too beautiful to have her name shortened. His body hardened at the thought of stroking her, murmuring her name as he tasted her sweet nectar—and heard his name on her lips as she came.

His gaze greedily roamed over her. She was bent at the waist, her hips balanced over the side of the open engine compartment, one leg braced on the edge, the other dangling for balance. She was as different today as she had been last night in the sports bra and red sequined gown.

She hadn't seen him yet.

S.E. SMITH

In the full light of day, she was… mesmerizing. Her dark auburn hair was twisted up in a messy bun, curls spilling like rebellious vines from pins barely clinging to order. His fingers itched to tug the pins free, just to watch that glorious mane fall around her shoulders.

Her skin was pale but kissed by the sun—more Mediterranean cream than porcelain. There was a smudge of engine grease on her cheek, just below one high cheekbone. It shouldn't have looked sensual. But on her, it did.

She muttered something he couldn't hear. With another unladylike growl, she twisted the wrench with a ferocious little grunt of triumph. The sound skittered down his spine like a challenge.

He recognized the instant she realized she wasn't alone anymore.

She turned, slowly, her eyes lifting and locking with his.

Wide. Green. And stunning.

Eyes that I could spend a lifetime drowning in, he thought with a sense of shock.

A beat of surprise flickered across her face, followed by something else—something that set his pulse kicking: delight. Her entire face lit up, and her mouth curved into a smile a man might kill to earn.

It hit him like a punch to the chest. Heat ricocheted through him, his body responding before his brain caught up. And then—

Pop! That was the only way to describe the sensual bubble building inside him.

"Oh! My baby!" she gasped, her eyes zeroing in on the tool bag like he was holding a kidnapped kitten instead of twenty pounds of steel.

He blinked. *Seriously?*

She practically cooed. "You found her! Come here, sweet thing. Mama missed you."

His lips flattened in disappointment. The sensual storm swirling inside him hiccupped and abruptly turned into annoyance. Not at her. At the damn tool bag.

Women cooed over diamonds. Not over socket sets!

She leaned over the railing and wiggled her fingers at him.

"Perfect timing! I need the 12-millimeter socket for a nut that refuses to admit defeat."

He stepped forward, climbed halfway up the ladder, and handed her the bag without a word. The weight transferred from his hand to hers—and in seconds, she had turned and vanished again into the trawler's belly. Just like in his dream.

Only this time, he wasn't going to let her slip away so easily.

He stood there, still on the ladder, unsure whether to laugh, groan, or shake her. He had brought her a peace offering. A chance to flirt. To banter. To maybe suggest lunch or wine.

Instead, she kissed her wrench kit with more passion than most of his dates.

"Brilliant," he muttered.

"Yes, having the right tool for the job really helps," she responded, completely unaware that she had figuratively pulled a step out from under his feet.

Alexandros Kallistratos—billionaire, shipping magnate, man who had entire cities change traffic routes for him—was now... ignored.

Deliberately.

Utterly.

For a socket and a greasy boat engine.

He eyed the hull of the trawler, noting the chipped paint, rust stains, and general grime. He was going to need new shoes after this. Possibly a tetanus shot.

A stubborn spark, like a tiny ember refusing to be extinguished, ignited in his chest. The unfamiliar terrain didn't deter him; he wasn't one to turn back from a challenge. And Danika Collins was utterly unpredictable, a wild card in the game of life.

He squared his shoulders and climbed the rest of the way up, stepping carefully onto the deck. She was crouched over the engine, one leg tucked beneath her, the other extended, her tank top clinging to her back as she twisted another bolt.

"Careful," he drawled. "You keep ignoring me, I might start thinking you're not madly in love with me."

She snorted without turning. "Trust me, Alex—if I ever go mad, you'll be the first to know."

He chuckled despite himself. "Alexandros. No one has *ever* referred to me as Alex."

She looked at him over her shoulder. He felt a flush of heat rise to his cheeks as she started at his polished shoes, moved up his legs—paused midway—before continuing up to his face. She raised an eyebrow, shrugged, and turned back to focus on the engine.

God help him.

He was in trouble.

And he liked it.

CHAPTER 5

*D*ani released the final nut with a satisfying click. Her triumph was short-lived, though. Her heart was thundering against her ribs, a frantic drumbeat threatening to burst free, making it difficult to breathe.

She hadn't expected to see him again; the surprise sent a jolt through her, a mix of excitement and trepidation. Not so soon. Definitely not at her place of work.

She had hoped her tool bag would magically reappear, sure—but the fantasy hadn't included Alexandros Kallistratos in designer slacks and a linen shirt, looking like a damn Greek god who'd decided to slum it for the day.

Dani tucked her chin and closed her eyes.

Count to ten. Breathe.

She could feel his gaze—steady, curious, and far too penetrating. His silence was louder than the hum of the music she had playing in the background. She wasn't ready to deal with him, with whatever this was crackling in the air between them like static clinging to her skin.

But avoiding him wasn't going to work—not with him standing there like temptation in human form.

Bracing a hand on the engine, she shifted to the side and swung her legs around, sliding onto the edge of the compartment. Her boots hit the floor with a muted thud, and she looked up, squinting at him in the filtered light streaming in through the open bay doors.

His expression was unreadable. Relaxed, maybe. Too relaxed.

"Thanks for the tool bag," she said, her voice dry. "But don't you have some billionaire things to do? Meetings to crash? Oceans to conquer? Wars to start?"

He smiled, slow and unapologetically. "Only the one I'm probably going to have with you. I want to see you again."

She blew out a breath, sending a wild curl bouncing against her cheek. "You came, you saw—" She mumbled.

"Ah, but I did not conquer—yet," he finished.

She snorted out a laugh and rolled her eyes at him. "Go away. I need to finish rebuilding the heads and carburetors on both engines. You know... normal Tuesday stuff. I don't have time to argue with you."

"Do you need a hand?"

Dani tilted her head, giving him a long, pointed look. "Your shirt probably costs more than this entire job. So, unless I'm mistaken and you bought it down at the neighborhood department store, I think you'd better stick to yachts and boardrooms."

His grin deepened at her sarcastic comment. She huffed out a breath when he folded his arms and leaned back against the side. She really hoped there wasn't anything disgusting on the aged wood that would leave an embarrassing reminder of his visit on the seat of his pants.

"I had Vito escorted off the yacht last night," he commented, breaking through her musing.

"Smart move. That alone should save you a mint in liability insurance."

Alexandros chuckled. Dani inhaled when a gentle ocean breeze flowed through the open doors. The scent of his cologne drifted toward her—subtle, clean, expensive. It curled around her senses, too inviting for her peace of mind.

"May I ask what brought you to Greece?"

Dani shrugged, her gaze falling to her tool bag. "Same as most people my age. Traveling. I liked it, so I've stayed on for a bit. I'm thinking it may be time to move on, though."

She kept her voice casual, carefully disinterested. The truth was too raw to hand over to a man like him—wrapped in wealth, charm, and good looks.

"And engine repair?" he asked. "That's not exactly something you pick up while backpacking through Europe."

Dani blinked, and—out of nowhere—laughter bubbled out of her. She shook her head, the absurdity of the moment finally sinking in.

Alexandros raised an eyebrow. "Did I say something funny?"

She looked up at him, amusement twinkling in her eyes. "I'm elbow-deep in a diesel engine. You're in slacks that cost more than my dock rent. And somehow, I'm pretty sure this is you flirting."

He made an indistinct sound in his throat, like a half-grunt, half-laugh. "I'll admit it—I've never had to work this hard to ask a woman out."

Her eyes widened slightly. "Is that what you're doing?"

"Yes," he said simply. "I am."

The honesty caught her off guard. It was quiet, confident—but not smug. She stared at the battered pouch, its wrenches and screwdrivers jutting out like stubby sea creatures—ugly, familiar, hers. The collection of tools had gotten her through more countries than her passport. She reached out and brushed the scuffed leather.

Before she could talk herself out of it, she met his eyes.

"There's a place called Taverna Thea," she said, her voice soft but firm. "Eight o'clock."

He hesitated before a frown creased his brow. "Wouldn't it be easier if I picked you up? Or we could have dinner on the yacht."

She gave him a look. "What, and risk another swim? I'd have to remember to wear a swimsuit and life vest this time."

He laughed. "Swimwear is optional, I promise. I'll keep you from sinking, and the only water involved would be in the pool, I promise.

It would also give us privacy. I'm afraid unless we went to a more exclusive restaurant, it would be a feast for the paparazzi."

"I imagine it would be difficult for you to blend in. Alright… but, dinner only. Don't go thinking that there is going to be anything else going on," she warned, pointing a finger at him.

Alexandros grinned like he'd just won the lottery. "I will be a perfect gentleman… unless you beg me not to be. Eight o'clock. Pier Five. I'll be waiting."

Dani couldn't believe she was agreeing. Maybe it was the honesty in his voice. Or maybe it was the way he hadn't pushed, just… waited. Whatever it was, it slipped past her defenses before she could stop it.

She bit her lip, following his movements as he swung his legs over the side and onto the ladder. She watched his retreating form, her heart fluttering somewhere between excitement and dread. No man had ever made her feel so exposed—not even Zayan. And that scared her more than anything.

It wasn't until he reached the edge of the building that realization struck her.

Pier Five.

He hadn't asked. He hadn't guessed. He'd known. Just like that, the ground beneath her no longer felt so solid anymore.

Dani's throat tightened.

The sense of déjà vu struck her unexpectedly. Like before… someone knowing too much, slipping past her walls, making her question if she'd ever really be safe again.

She forced the thought away, but it clung like an oil smear beneath her skin. She wasn't a naive kid anymore. Alexandros Kallistratos differed from most of the guys she met—from Zayan.

Maybe realizing that was what scared her the most.

FROM THE SHADOWED side of a white cargo van, a man stood silent, motionless but for the slow rise and fall of his chest.

The midmorning sun glinted off the gleaming silver curves of the

Bentley Continental GT as it rolled out of the boatyard, kicking up a swirl of dust in its wake. The man's eyes—dark and sharp as a hawk's—tracked the luxury vehicle until it turned the corner and disappeared.

A half-million euro car, he mused with a smirk.

It fit the arrogant bastard behind the wheel.

His gaze slid back to the cavernous boat bay across the lot. The clang of metal and muffled curses drifted from the shadows—sounds as familiar to him as blood and salt. It was a world he understood—oil, sweat, effort. The life that wore down a man's hands, spine, and dreams.

And there she was.

Dani Collins.

The name curled in his mind, not with affection—but with the bitter taste of unfinished business. His dark eyes narrowed as he studied her. The sneer pulled at the scar on his upper lip.

She took everything that mattered to me. Now, I'll take everything back—and with interest.

Dani hadn't seen him—probably wouldn't recognize him if she did. He had changed a lot since they had last seen each other.

No, she hadn't seen him—not yet, but she would. He'd first caught sight of her three weeks ago, bent over the hull of a fishing boat near the docks, her auburn curls tumbling from beneath a bandana, grease on her cheek, laughing at something a dockhand was saying.

The sound of her laughter had nearly stopped his heart.

It had taken him years.

Years of crawling his way across continents. Years of backbreaking labor on cargo ships, hauling nets on trawlers, pretending to be invisible while the salt and sun stole the softness from his skin and the last remnants of his youth.

But he'd found her—and she was more beautiful today than she had been four years ago.

His discovery had been by chance, yes—but the gods had smiled on him. At last.

And now… now she would pay.

The plan formed with quiet precision in his mind. He'd already started the groundwork. New identification. A false name in the port registry. Connections with men who wouldn't ask questions when he needed to disappear. All he needed was time—and patience.

And he had both in abundance.

His gaze swept over the bay again. Dani's silhouette moved within the shadows, her voice carrying as she spoke to someone—laughing again.

That laughter would stop soon enough.

She didn't even know it yet, but she had just become the most valuable pawn in a game that would end in wealth, vengeance... and blood.

Because Alexandros Kallistratos had just made her even more important.

His smile widened, but it held no warmth—only yellowed teeth and cruelty.

He would take her... while bleeding the billionaire for a few of his millions of euros. And when it was done, when the ransom was in hand and the trail cold...

He would have his revenge. Not just for the scandal. Not just for the whispers and the exile and the humiliation. But for what she cost him.

"The gods always repay betrayal," he whispered to no one, the phrase bitter on his tongue.

And he? He had waited long enough to collect.

She would know it was him before the end.

He slid into the driver's seat of the van and watched.

Soon, he promised himself.

Very soon.

THE AXOPAR 37 Sun-Top purred beneath Alexandros as Demetrius eased it into the marina's outer channel. The sleek Scandinavian craft sliced cleanly through the early evening tide, its matte hull catching soft flickers of sunset gold. The engine rumbled low, steady—controlled power beneath his feet. Alexandros didn't notice the breeze off the sea or the sting of salt in the air.

His focus was entirely on the woman standing barefoot at the edge of *The Gentle Breeze.*

She turned at the sound of their approach, sunlight kissing her face, and smiled.

It wasn't a polite smile. It wasn't measured or practiced or held back. It was delighted—utterly unguarded—and it hit him like a damn lightning strike.

She wore a loose peasant blouse the color of sea glass, the sleeves fluttering in the breeze. Her skirt flowed around her legs like a living thing, patterned in tiny, embroidered wildflowers that looked like they'd been pressed by hand. His gaze dropped to her bare feet. Dainty, with a series of beaded ankle bracelets wrapped around one.

He'd never picked up a date who was barefoot.

And certainly never one who made his mouth go dry as she grabbed a line, hitched up her skirt, and climbed onto the dock with effortless grace.

A sound hissed from between his teeth, unbidden.

Demetrius chuckled beside him, low and amused. "I'm telling you —she's trouble."

Alexandros didn't look at him. His gaze was locked on Dani as she walked toward them, the sway of her hips unintentional, unstudied. She was all motion and contradiction—sunlight and steel, softness wrapped around something unbreakable.

She stopped at the edge of the speedboat and looked down at him with a teasing glint in her eyes.

"You pick your dates up by boat?" she asked, grinning. "And not a minute late. I'm impressed."

Alexandros rose to meet her, every inch of him taut with awareness. "Only the extraordinary ones."

He reached up, his hands sliding around her waist. The moment his fingers brushed her sides, fire shot through his veins. Her breath caught—he felt it. Saw the flicker in her eyes. The way they dilated.

Her hands tightened slightly on his shoulders before trailing down his chest as he lowered her into the boat.

He nearly groaned at the contact.

Control. He needed control.

"You're stronger than I expected," she reflected, her breath warm and teasing against his ear.

His eyes flashed as the tendrils of desire flamed. He reluctantly released her before guiding her toward the cushioned rear bench. She swept a loose curl from her face and tilted her head at him. The light breeze tugged at her skirt and blouse.

"You okay with the wind?" he asked, wanting a reason—any reason —to pull her closer.

Her eyes sparkled. "Are you kidding? This is fabulous."

She turned to Demetrius and offered a cheerful, "Hi. You're Demetrius, right? I didn't know you doubled as a captain when you aren't following unsuspecting girls around. Sweet ride, by the way. What kind of motor does this thing have?"

Demetrius's mouth curved into a smile as he responded, describing the twin Mercury Verado 350s and the boat's performance specs. She leaned forward, totally absorbed, tossing questions like she belonged in a marina more than any luxury villa. Alexandros watched the way she asked about torque curves and fuel economy, utterly at ease—no performance, no pretense.

She didn't care about appearances.

She cared about how things worked.

And that was more dangerous than beauty.

Because he'd met dozens—hundreds—of beautiful women. But none who made him want to know why they were the way they were. None who made him feel like one wrong move might scare them away… and leave him chasing the ghost of what could have been.

He dropped into the seat beside her, letting the roar of the water mask the chaos in his chest.

He knew he was in trouble last night, but tonight—tonight, he knew deep down that this woman was an extraordinary find, one that there was no way he was going to let slip through his fingers.

He vaguely wondered what it might feel like—to be seen, not as a Kallistratos, but as a man. Just a man. It was a novel feeling that Dani didn't see him for his money, power, and status.

Unless she is one hell of an actress, he mused before dismissing the idea.

No, there was no pretense with Dani.

What unsettled him the most was that for once, he didn't care about his meticulously laid plans for the future. He had known he would marry one day, have the prerequisite one or two children that were expected, and if he was lucky, tolerate the prison he imagined marriage to be. But with Dani, something told him every day would be an adventure that he would wake up and look forward to—and every night a thrill he'd never grow tired of exploring.

CHAPTER 6

The yacht grew larger with every second, sleek and regal as it waited on the water like a crown jewel of the Aegean.

Dani sat in the stern of the Axopar, her head tilted back, the wind teasing the ends of her scarf and the hem of her skirt. Alexandros sat next to her, one arm lazily draped around her waist, his hand warm and solid against her hip. He hadn't asked—he'd just pulled her back against him as the boat cut across the bay—and to her own surprise; she hadn't resisted.

In fact, she hadn't wanted to. Which is what really surprised her. His touch felt different from when Carlos touched her—or at least the way she reacted to him wasn't the same. She felt nothing but friend-ship with the naughty Spaniard who loved to tease and flirt with any woman close by. With Alexandros, something primal stirred in her. His scent, his touch, his smile—everything about him pulled her in, made her want to melt into him.

He's like the sun and water, she thought with a sigh of contentment.

Her nervousness wasn't because of him. Not exactly. It was the way her feelings kept expanding in directions she hadn't expected—and definitely didn't feel ready for. There was something terrifying in the ease of it all. The way she leaned back against his chest without hesitation. The way she felt... safe.

The sun dipped low on the horizon, streaking the sky with honey-gold and dusky rose—like a Byzantine fresco kissed by the gods. Its reflection shimmered across the waves like scattered diamonds. Onshore, whitewashed buildings hugged the curves of the hills, their terracotta roofs glowing in the last light. The scent of sea spray, sun-warmed salt, and Alexandros's cologne wrapped around her like a dream she wasn't ready to wake from.

She sighed, letting herself relax a little more, her muscles loosening as the wind threaded through the gauzy scarf tied around her hair.

Alexandros leaned in slightly. "What are you thinking?"

"This," she murmured, her voice soft with wonder. She lifted one hand and gestured toward the sky, the water, the world around them. "Just... how lucky I am. To be here. To be alive. To be living like this. In this time and place."

She could feel his curious smile against her shoulder.

"Not just lucky to be on a boat with a ridiculously handsome billionaire who finds you fascinating?" he teased, his voice low and warm in her ear.

She chuckled, but didn't turn around. "That's just a bonus, or a liability—depending on how you look at it."

"Oh? I think I would prefer it to be a bonus."

"I'm sure," she said, grinning now, "I'm not denying you're easy on the eyes. But I meant what I said. I'm lucky to be a woman—right now, in this time. I don't take that for granted."

There was a pause. "What do you mean?"

She shifted slightly so she could glance up at him over her shoulder. "If I'd been born even twenty years earlier, I don't think I could've done half of what I've done. Marine engine repair? That was a boys' club for a long time—and still kind of is."

His brow furrowed. "I never thought about that. That what you do might be difficult... from a female point of view."

She chuckled. "Exactly. Most guys don't think about it—and I prefer it that way. I don't want special treatment—I just want to be allowed to do what I love without having to prove I belong every damn day."

"Is it still difficult?" he asked.

"Sometimes." Her smile turned wry. "Case in point—jerks like Vito who think I'm part of the perks package."

His arm tightened slightly. "I owe you an apology for that. I allowed Vito the use of the yacht as a favor to his stepsister, Gina. That was a mistake. One I won't repeat."

She raised an eyebrow. "Was that before or after your 'discussion' with him?"

"After," he said, the corner of his mouth twitching. "Though I suppose the timing is debatable."

Dani laughed. "Is that why he not only paid my bill but tripled it?"

Alexandros shrugged with exaggerated innocence. "Maybe."

She nudged his leg with her bare foot. "You're terrible—but I won't turn down the money."

"You said that being here was also a liability. How so?"

"Because you're dangerous, and I try to limit my danger content," she quipped.

"And how am I dangerous?" he inquired, his warm breath caressing her exposed neck and sending goosebumps across her skin.

"You're a temporary lapse in judgment," she replied, her gaze flicking away. "Like skipping the frying pan and diving straight into the bonfire."

"So... you feel this chemistry, as well," he said, his voice laced with satisfaction.

Oh yes, I feel it. But acting on it is another thing, she thought with fierce determination.

She knew what he wanted—her, messy sheets, a night, maybe two if she was lucky, followed by a nice parting gift and a promise to call that never comes.

Or worse.

She pushed down the memories of betrayal. There was nothing

like seeing the man she thought she loved wrapped in the embrace of another woman.

Or two, or three.

A gentle silence stretched between them, filled with the rush of the wind and the rhythmic chop of waves beneath the hull. His arm stayed around her, steady and warm, and she didn't move away. Couldn't.

It felt too good to be held like this—without expectations, without pressure. Just... held.

She tilted her head, letting it rest against his shoulder—not for long, but long enough to pretend, just for a breath, that it was okay to want this. The distant lights of the yacht glowed like fireflies ahead, drawing closer with every second.

And somewhere inside her, another piece of resistance slipped loose.

That scared her.

Not because she didn't trust him—but because she didn't trust herself. Not when everything inside her was starting to ache for more.

She'd survived by staying one step ahead, by never getting too comfortable, too attached, too trusting. But here she was, tucked into a man she had met for the first time last night. Who made her laugh—and whose arms made her feel like they were supposed to be wrapped around her.

If she let herself believe in love again—even for a moment—then losing it wouldn't just break her. It would mean she'd handed over the pieces herself.

Her fingers curled slightly on her lap.

Careful, Dani.

Don't fall too fast.

Don't fall at all.

But the voice in her head was already quieter than it should've been. And the worst part? Some traitorous part of her already wanted to stay.

Not just tonight. Longer.

～

THE MOMENT the Axopar pulled alongside the yacht, Alexandros stood and extended his hand. The lights from the deck cast a soft golden glow across the water, catching the shifting colors of dusk still clinging to the horizon. Dani looked up at him, her eyes unreadable—but she didn't hesitate. Her fingers slid into his, small and warm, her trust disarming in a way nothing else could have been.

He helped her up, keeping her close as they stepped onto the yacht's polished deck. The subtle sway beneath their feet felt like the sea itself was holding its breath.

When they entered the main salon, he saw the exact moment Dani noticed the table.

It wasn't elaborate—just a crisp white cloth, two elegant place settings, and a candle flickering inside a hurricane lamp. But it was intimate. Thoughtful. Intentional.

Her lips curved, the corners of her mouth quirking with quiet amusement. Her gaze moved to his as one eyebrow arched in silent question.

Her fingers trailed across the cloth—slow, light, like a lover's touch.

His body responded instantly.

Desire flared hot and fast, uncoiling in his gut and racing through his veins. He wanted her. Craved her. Not just the way she moved or looked—but the way she felt. Her laughter. Her strength. Her intelligence. Her fire. He wanted to discover every layer, to strip her bare in every sense and find out what made Danika Collins burn.

A flicker of heat crossed her face as her gaze caught his.

She stilled.

Alexandros didn't move, barely breathed, knowing she saw it—the reflection of that hunger in his eyes. He didn't hide the evidence of his arousal pressing against the front of his slacks.

Her gaze dipped, lingered, then flicked back up to meet his—steady, curious… and something more. Unspoken. Waiting.

She turned and walked to the rail, resting her palms against the polished wood as she looked out across the sea. Her silhouette was painted in the dim golden light, a halo of warmth from the salon spilling onto the deck.

"Would you like something to drink?" he asked, his voice husky with restraint.

She glanced over her shoulder, a soft smile playing on her lips. "Just water. Non-sparkle."

He tilted his head. "Non-sparkle?"

"I'm not much of a drinker, and I hate the carbonated stuff," she said with a shrug. "I never acquired a taste for wine."

He retrieved a bottle of chilled spring water from the bar and poured it into a crystal glass before offering it to her. As she took it, her fingers brushed his again—another electric jolt.

He set his own wine down, exhaled sharply, and reached for the scarf tied around her hair.

She turned to face him, curiosity sparking in her eyes.

He moved slowly.

Gently.

Unwrapping her like a gift he wasn't sure he deserved.

The scarf came away first, slipping from her hair like silk through his fingers. Her lips parted when he found the pins hidden beneath and removed them one by one, each removal a dance of seduction. Her hair tumbled down in a cascade of auburn waves, catching the candlelight and stealing his breath.

"*Exóplaísi*," he whispered. Enchanting.

She blinked up at him, but said nothing as he took her glass and set it aside. His hand slid along the curve of her waist, drawing her closer. Her breath hitched, and he felt the tension in her—not resistance, but anticipation.

He paused.

Giving her time.

Giving her a choice.

Dani lifted her hands to his chest, her fingers splaying over the fine linen of his shirt. She didn't push him away. She slid them upward—slow, deliberate—until her palms rested over his heart.

It thundered beneath her touch.

She rose on her toes and met him halfway.

The kiss was slow.

Searching.

It wasn't rushed—not yet.

It was reverent.

A question and an answer all at once.

Her lips were soft and warm, molding to his. Her hands moved to his shoulders, curling there, holding on as if the world might shift beneath them. His own hands framed her face, angling her gently, deepening the kiss, coaxing her to open to him.

When she did, it shattered him.

Everything else—his past, his plans, the image of the life he thought he wanted—fell away like smoke on the sea air.

She tasted of salt and wind and something wild he hadn't realized he'd been missing.

He broke the kiss with a groan, his forehead resting against hers, his breathing ragged.

"Danika," he murmured.

Her name was like a vow and a prayer on his tongue.

She didn't answer. Just leaned into him, her eyes closed, her body flush against his, as if she wasn't ready to let go of the moment either.

And neither was he.

Because in that single kiss, he knew.

She was different.

She was real.

And she was destined to be his.

THE SUBTLE CLICK of the door opening broke the spell. Dani pulled back, her breath catching, her cheeks blooming into a flush of delicate pink. Alexandros stepped back as she turned, quickly tucking loose strands of hair behind her ear. She reached for her glass of water, masking the tremor in her fingers as the steward entered with the quiet confidence of someone well-trained in discretion.

Alexandros nodded to the man to begin serving.

"I'll let you know when we're ready for the second course," he said calmly.

The steward inclined his head and moved to set the appetizers onto the table.

Alexandros crossed the room and pulled out a chair for Dani. She slid into it gracefully, murmuring a soft, "Thank you," without meeting his gaze.

He waited until she was seated before circling to the opposite side and taking his own chair.

The steward poured him a fresh glass of wine, bowed again, and disappeared as quietly as he'd come.

Dani took a sip of her water, then met his eyes—mischief dancing in hers. "So," she said, leaning back slightly. "What did your background report say about me?"

He almost choked on his first sip of wine. A slash of heat rushed to his cheeks—not entirely from the wine—and he cleared his throat, setting the glass down.

"I'm not sure what you mean," he replied, aiming for casual, but her amused expression told him she wasn't buying it.

She lifted an eyebrow. "You called me Danika. I never told you that. In fact, the only person who *ever* called me that was my grandmother. And after last night's surprise dive off your yacht, I'd have done the same thing. I'm guessing your lawyers weren't thrilled about the liability."

Her tone was light, teasing, but her eyes were too sharp to be anything but serious.

He gave a short, reluctant laugh. "I might have wanted to know who you were before inviting you aboard again."

She grinned. "Smart man."

"Should I be worried about that liability?" he asked, playing along.

Her smile wavered as she stared back at him. "Only about the fire you started inside me," she confessed in a soft voice.

The moment the words slipped out, her eyes widened, and color flooded her cheeks. She looked away quickly, focusing on the cutlery like it held state secrets.

Alexandros leaned forward, elbows braced on the table, his voice low. "You know... you literally brought me to my knees the first time we met."

She glanced up, a question in her eyes.

"I can honestly say," he continued, "no other woman has ever done that."

Her lips parted, the air between them shifting. She laughed, soft and surprised, the tension easing.

Over dinner, their conversation unfolded like a slow dance—organic, teasing, layered. The food was impeccable—fresh grilled fish with lemon and herbs, warm bread, marinated olives, roasted vegetables—but Alexandros barely noticed what he was eating.

Dani challenged him.

They debated current events with equal fervor—she had strong opinions about renewable energy, while he argued the limitations of infrastructure and real-world logistics. She listened intently, cut in without apology, and countered his points with wit and facts. She didn't back down—and she didn't get defensive when he didn't agree.

He found it exhilarating.

She spoke with passion, even when they disagreed, and he realized he'd never had this kind of conversation with a woman at dinner. Usually it was small talk, compliments, and polite laughter.

This? This was real.

He wasn't sure how the topic ended up shifting to one he normally avoided at all costs.

Discussions of love, marriage, and lifelong commitment were strictly off-limits, a taboo subject shrouded in unspoken rules. To his surprise, the words tumbled out of his mouth before he could stop them, a realization that shocked even him.

"I'm not sure I believe in love," he admitted, swirling the dark red wine, the ruby liquid catching the dim light, and avoiding her questioning gaze. "Not... the kind that lasts. From my experience, it is a fleeting emotion."

"What about your parents? Do they love each other?" she asked.

He chuckled. "Their marriage was an arranged one. I would say they are the closest thing to love that I have seen. My mother teases that they started out as strangers who slowly fell in love."

"Isn't that how it begins for everyone? We are all strangers—you and I—but, the longer we spend together the more we get to know each other. I'm not saying that we're falling in love or anything like that, but that is how it begins. My parents always said there are five things that a couple has to agree on if they are to have a strong, successful marriage."

He paused and lifted his glass. "Five things?" he repeated, leaning forward. "What are the mythical five things that guarantee eternal bliss?

She leaned her elbows on the table and studied him. "Well, money."

He lifted an eyebrow and gave her a cynical nod. "Ah, yes. The most important element."

She shook her head. "No, not the most important, but necessary. It isn't about how much, or who has it. It's about how to spend it, invest it. Things like that. If I balance the checkbook, or do you? If we have separate or joint accounts. It's about trusting each other."

"Go on," he encouraged.

"Okay. There's the in-laws."

"How do in-laws factor into a marriage?" he asked, growing intrigued.

"Well, you can love them—or hate them—but, in the end, the relationship is between you and your spouse. Do you go to one house for this holiday and the other for the next? If you or your spouse doesn't get along with them, how do you handle that? Is there a reason, and will you support your spouse? It may mean compromising, but there has to be an understanding."

"This seems like a very intense list," he commented dryly.

He was fascinated by factors that he had never considered. He wondered if any of these were part of a prenup. It would be interesting to see how his lawyers would deal with the 'in-law' factor.

She nodded, completely serious. "Better to know where you stand before you marry than after. The next one is religion. This one can be tricky. Are you religious? What if your spouse isn't? What if your spouse's religion is restrictive to you?"

"I can see where that one could cause issues. I'm not, by the way—religious. Next on your list," he said.

She smiled and bowed her head. "The next is children. What if one of you doesn't want any? What if one of you can't have children? What if one of you wants ten kids and the other only wants two?"

"I would have to bow to my imaginary wife's desires on numbers, but—yes, one day, I would like to have a child or two. As long as it is possible," he amended.

"Yeah," she said softly. "Someday, a couple would be nice."

The more she spoke, the more he couldn't stop thinking about her —as his imaginary wife. He studied her, visualizing her body changing, growing round with his child. The vision sent an unexpected shaft of longing through him.

He silently cursed. He had never had a desire to see any of his previous lovers pregnant. Hell, unless they could make a few million off him, none of them wanted anything to do with children. Children were noisy, messy, and far too demanding.

"And the last?" he asked, his throat tight as he continued picturing holding Dani and feeling his child growing inside her.

She fought a grin. "Sex."

The last one surprised him, and he frowned. "Sex? Isn't that already included in the marriage contract?"

She laughed. "Yes, but there's a *lot* of gray area in those three letters."

"Such as?"

He knew he was in trouble when that mischievous twinkle appeared in her eyes again. "Well, there is how often do you do it?"

"Daily—multiple times," he said, his voice dropping.

"How—?" Her voice faded, and she waved her hand towards him.

"What does this mean? How—?" and he mimicked her hand wave.

She bit her lip before running her tongue over it. "In what positions? How do you like it? Mission style?" she asked, before her eyes dropped to his lips. "Or do you like to experiment? Try different things? Explore ways to heighten your connection? Do-do you like it exciting?"

"Always, what about you?" he asked, his body on fire. "What about you, Danika? How do you like it?

"I don't know," she said, her voice laced with amusement. "I've never... been with anyone." Her gaze held his, an impish twinkle in them as she continued, "I guess I'll find out when I do."

Shock coursed through him. He couldn't have heard her correctly. Did she just admit that she was still a—virgin? His gaze swept over her beautiful face. Her magnificent hair. Her curves.

He blinked. Once. Twice. "You... have never been with a man?"

"Never," she said with a shrug. "Amazing, huh?"

He sat frozen, his mind still reeling.

"Oh, look! Dessert!" she chirped, as if she hadn't just upended his entire reality.

Her sweet smile lingered as he choked on more than just his wine.

CHAPTER 7

*A*s dessert arrived—local figs soaked in honey and topped with fresh cream—the air between them shimmered with something new. It was more than lust—stronger than any attraction he'd known. It left him reeling. He wanted to dive into where these new, unfamiliar emotions would take him.

He found himself memorizing everything: the cadence of her voice, the glint of mischief when she teased him, the way her fingers danced along her glass when she was thinking. He wanted to know what made her smile, what made her afraid, what dreams she still hadn't chased.

Tonight had shown him something he hadn't realized he was looking for.

And she was sitting right across the table.

"I knew I would marry one day. I believed I'd go through the motions—when the timing was convenient. It always felt like an obligation—something I was expected to do, not something I would choose for myself. Not for love, but to meet expectations."

Dani studied him for a long moment. She said softly, "I believe in love—true love. Deeply."

He looked up. There was a hesitant note in her voice.

She smiled—not wistfully, but with a kind of quiet certainty. "My grandparents had it. That connection. I would see it when they looked across a room. The way their eyes searched for each other. Even after my grandmother died, Gramps still looks for her." Her voice faltered, just for a beat. "My parents were the same."

He tilted his head. "How do they feel about your being here? In another country, alone?"

She lowered her eyes. Her smile faltered. She hesitated—just a breath, a blink—and everything changed.

"My folks were killed in a plane crash when I was fifteen."

His chest tightened as the image hit him.

She stared down at the napkin on her lap, then folded it once, twice. Her voice, when it came again, was steady—but quieter. "It's just Gramps and me now. He's amazing. He taught me how to hold a wrench before I could ride a bike. He used to tell me I could fix anything—engines, hearts, the world."

Alexandros reached across the table without thinking, brushing his fingers lightly over hers.

She looked up, startled by the touch, but didn't pull away.

"I'm sorry," he said softly. "Fifteen is… that's too young. Even at twenty-nine, I still look to my parents for guidance."

Dani gave a wobbly smile. "It was. But you keep going, you know? Because you have to. And eventually, you learn to live with the quiet."

He wanted to reach for her then, to pull her into his arms and hold her until she forgot the grief etched into her memory. But he gave her what she seemed to need most: his attention. His silence. His steady presence.

"You've lived more lives than most people twice your age," he said after a moment.

She blinked at him. "What makes you say that?"

"You have stories behind your eyes," he said simply. "You don't flinch when things get real. You lean in. Most people don't."

Dani gave him a look that was part challenge, part gratitude. "You're not what I expected."

He chuckled. "Good or bad?"

"I'm still deciding—but… I think… mostly good. Very, very good."

"I want to hold you, Danika," he murmured, rising from his chair while still retaining her hand.

She didn't resist.

When she stepped into his arms, it felt like the world stilled.

He didn't kiss her—not yet. He just held her, her cheek nestled against his heart, as if that was where she had always belonged. Her warmth seeped into him.

Outside, waves lapped gently against the hull. Inside, all he could hear was the steady rhythm of her breath.

She fit against him in a way that made no logical sense. But in that moment, it felt right.

Whatever was happening between them wasn't casual. It was more.

And he knew it.

She was like a wild creature—graceful, guarded, wary.

Afraid to trust her heart.

And for the first time in his life, he wanted to earn that trust.

She was afraid to trust her heart—just as I'd never believed I had one worth giving.

DANI STOOD at the edge of the dock, watching the speedboat idling back out into the channel as Demetrius guided it across the moonlit bay. The wind played with the ends of her scarf, tugging to be free. At the stern of the boat, Alexandros stood with his hands in his pockets, watching her as he had done every night for the past four nights—until distance swallowed him from view.

She pressed her palm to her chest, right where her heart thudded like a hammer wrapped in velvet.

Each night had been more romantic than the last, but tonight had been one of the most thrilling, frustrating, terrifyingly wonderful nights of her life.

She knew deep down that she was in danger of completely, hopelessly, terrifyingly falling in love with Alexandros Kallistratos if she wasn't careful.

She turned from the dock and started back toward the *Gentle Breeze*, her bare feet silent against the wooden planks. Her lips were curved in a smile she couldn't hide, her body felt like it was filled with warm champagne bubbles, and her heart... her heart felt like it was no longer her own.

He had asked her to stay, as he had done each night before, but there had been something different about his request tonight. For one irrational, aching second, she had almost said yes. If he had kissed her one more time, if he'd lingered just a moment longer, her resolve would have shattered.

But he hadn't kissed her again.

He hadn't pressed.

He had simply... let her go.

That restraint—his quiet, honorable respect—made her respect him a hundred times more.

She reached the trawler and climbed aboard, still humming under her breath. Unlocking the double doors to the salon, she stepped inside, closed the doors, and locked them again behind her. The gentle scent of lavender she had growing in pots and the teak oil polish used on the wood greeted her like home. She twirled across the room, keys landing with a clink on the counter, before flopping onto the bench seat in a daze of contentment.

Dani started when her phone suddenly buzzed.

She glanced at the screen and laughed softly. Stuart.

She answered with a bright, "Hi, Gramps!"

His familiar chuckle rumbled through the line. "There's my girl. I was wondering if you were still floating around out there or if some swarthy Greek sailor had swept you off your feet."

She grinned and stretched out, one arm behind her head. "Oh, I'm floating alright... figuratively and literally."

He paused. "That sounds suspiciously dreamy."

"It was... a good day," she said, and then quieter, "and a really magical evening."

"Well now," Stuart said, warmth laced with curiosity, "Do tell—as long as it is something my old ears can hear and my old heart can handle."

Dani told him everything—about the job, the tools, the sea, and finally, Alexandros. Her voice softened, grew hesitant.

"I think... I might be falling for him, Gramps. Is it real? This doesn't... feel like the last time."

There was a long beat of silence before her grandfather spoke. His voice, when it came, was lower, gruffer. "The first time I saw your grandmother, she was standing on a street corner in a yellow dress and holding a bouquet of sunflowers. She smiled at me like she knew me... and damn if my heart didn't leap right out of my chest."

Dani swallowed, touched.

"How did you know?" she asked, her voice barely above a whisper.

"You don't always know with your head. Sometimes your soul knows before your mind catches up. Sometimes, two souls that have been searching through time just... hear each other. Like echoes calling across the stars."

Dani blinked, tears slipping down her cheeks. "Gramps, I didn't know you were such a romantic."

"I wasn't—until that day," he said gently. "She made me believe in things I didn't even know I needed. Even after all this time... I still believe I'll see her again."

She bit her lip, touched to her core. "What do I do?"

There was a pause, then, "What does your gut tell you, sweetheart?"

Dani stared up at the ceiling, the beams overhead bathed in moonlight. "It tells me to trust him. But I'm scared, Gramps. What if he breaks my heart?"

"Then at least you gave it a chance to beat for something that mattered. You can't live your life in fear, Dani. Love's a risk. But it's the only thing worth the bruises."

She smiled, wiped her eyes. "You're a smart man, Stuart Bouras."

"You take after me."

They spoke a little longer before she whispered, "Goodnight, Gramps."

"Goodnight, pumpkin. Sweet dreams."

She hung up, laying the phone on her chest for a moment before slipping it into her pocket. The clouds drifted outside the salon windows, their soft gray shadows stretching across the sky. Her thoughts swirled, too tangled for sleep.

With a sigh, she stood and turned toward the narrow stairwell leading below deck.

And froze.

A dark shape stood in the shadows—just beyond the edge of the moonlight. It hadn't been there a second ago.

Her heart stuttered, her breath caught, her instincts screamed before her mind could react.

"Who—?" she started, but didn't finish.

The shadow lunged. Arms—strong, thick, unbreakable—wrapped around her from behind. A hand clamped over her mouth, cutting off her scream.

Her vision swam as she kicked, clawed—but he didn't budge. Her terror exploded when he pressed a rag to her face. An acrid and chemical burning filled her nostrils.

No!

She twisted, trying to scream, but the cloth cut off her breath. Her vision blurred.

Her heart pounded with terror.

A voice, hot and hateful, in her ear.

"Did you miss me, *azziz?*"

No! Please... no, she thought as the world slipped sideways.

Before darkness pulled her down into its greedy realm.

THE RHYTHMIC THUMP of the helicopter blades echoed across the rooftop helipad as the sleek black aircraft touched down atop the gleaming steel-and-glass tower in the heart of Athens. The rising sun painted the Acropolis in golden hues in the distance, but Alexandros barely spared it a glance. His mind was miles away—back onboard the *Kallistratos Challenge*, on a dock bathed in moonlight, with a woman who had turned his world upside down.

He stepped out of the chopper, his custom leather shoes clicking against the polished landing pad. The sharp Mediterranean wind tugged at his open collar and the edges of his tailored navy jacket.

"Welcome back, sir," Julius greeted, walking briskly beside him. The ever-efficient PA fell in step without missing a beat, tablet already in hand. "Your brother has called twice. Your father once. And you've missed four meetings, two strategy calls, and I took the initiative when I didn't hear from you to reschedule your breakfast with the Norwegian delegation."

Alexandros grunted, his eyes fixed ahead as they crossed the rooftop terrace and entered the private elevator.

"Tell the Norwegians I'll host them for lunch," he said absently. "With their pick of wine from the cellar. And send my apologies to the minister."

"Yes, sir. And the Dryfuss deal—"

"Later," Alexandros cut in, his voice low but final.

Julius hesitated. "Very well."

The elevator descended with a soft hum, opening directly into the penthouse-level executive suite of Kallistratos International. Floor-to-ceiling windows offered an uninterrupted view of Athens awakening below—traffic flowing like silver veins, marble monuments rising between ultra-modern buildings.

But Alexandros saw none of it. All he saw was Dani.

Her smile as she'd watched him leave. Her sun-kissed skin. The delicate lines of her collarbone beneath that loose peasant blouse.

I still don't know what her favorite color is, he thought. *Or whether she prefers sunrise to sunset. What she dreams about when she's alone. But I'll find out. I'll learn every inch of her... body and soul.*

He didn't realize Julius had stopped speaking until the man cleared his throat.

"My apologies," Alexandros muttered. "Tell legal I'll join the meeting in thirty. Come prepared."

Julius gave a curt nod. "Understood."

Alexandros crossed the expansive office and closed the door behind him. The silence that followed was thick and deliberate—his fortress, his control. But this morning, the silence was threaded with impatience.

He pulled out his phone and dialed his brother, Theo.

The line barely rang once.

"Where the hell have you been?" Theo barked, his voice clipped with irritation. "Gina cornered me at that rooftop club in Kolonaki last night, going on about you kicking her stepbrother off your yacht. And that's not even the worst of it—the Dryfuss deal is this close to going sideways."

Alexandros ran a hand through his hair and leaned back against the edge of his desk, grinning despite himself. "Would it help if I told you I seriously considered tying an anchor around Vito's neck before tossing him overboard?"

Theo laughed, despite his obvious annoyance. "That would've made my night a hell of a lot easier."

"She's not one of my lovers," Alexandros said firmly. "Despite what Gina wants."

"Then tell her. Before I have to hear about it again."

A pause before Theo added, "So...what's the story? Vito was going on and on about some mechanic throwing herself overboard after making a scene."

"She didn't make a scene—well, she did, but she had a right to. Vito locked her in my stateroom," Alexandros replied, the smile returning to his lips. "And yes, she escaped—after punching me in the groin."

"She did *what*?! She attacked you? And what do you mean, she jumped overboard? At night?" Theo chuckled.

"Yes. Then, she had the nerve to ask if I was nuts for following her. Her name is Dani. I've never met a woman like her before, Theo. She is magnificent."

There was another pause. Theo chuckled and released a low whistle. "Dani, huh? You sound... serious."

Alexandros turned toward the windows, eyes scanning the horizon without seeing it. "I am. She's... smart. Gorgeous. Funny. Real. And I want her. All of her."

"Damn," Theo muttered. "And here I thought we agreed neither of us did serious."

"I didn't. Until her."

Silence stretched between the brothers for a beat before they shifted back into business mode, breaking down the Dryfuss merger with sharp efficiency. Numbers, projections, liabilities. But even as they strategized, Alexandros's mind kept drifting back to Dani's smile.

Before they ended the call, Theo asked, "When are you introducing her to the family?"

"This weekend. At the estate."

"You're bringing a woman home?" Theo sounded stunned. "To Syros?"

"Yes," Alexandros said. "I told you, she's different. I want you, Mother, and Father to meet her."

"I'll be there."

After hanging up, Alexandros immediately called his father.

Christos Kallistratos answered in his usual baritone, steady and commanding. "Alexandros. About the Dryfuss issue—"

"Handled. Theo and I are coordinating. I meet with Legal in... fifteen minutes. Don't worry. It will go through."

There was a brief silence. "What is going on with Gina? Apollo and Dorothea dropped in unexpectedly for dinner last night. They would really like to see an announcement."

"I will not be pressured into any of Gina or her parent's charades. It is nothing but a wishful dream on their part. I imagine they would like to get rid of the monster they have created."

Christos sighed. "Gina has been feeding them a line that your engagement is imminent. Your mother and I pretended to be surprised by the information and told them we hadn't heard anything."

"She is dreaming. There never has, nor will there ever be, anything between Gina and me. She still harbors a belief from when we were kids and you and Apollo jokingly mentioned we would make a good match. She'll get over it."

"Yes, your mother tends to remind me about that unfortunate conversation whenever Apollo and Dorothea visit," Christos grumbled. "Gina's not the type to get over things. She tends to let things fester. I'll have another word with Apollo."

"I'm aware. You needn't bother. I'll deal with Gina once and for all," Alexandros said before he hesitated. "I wanted to let you know... I'll be at the villa on Syros this weekend. And I'll be bringing a guest."

His father's voice held a flicker of interest. "A guest?"

"A woman. A very special one."

Another pause. Then, with mild surprise, "Your mother will be delighted. You've never brought a woman to meet us, much less to our family home."

"I know," Alexandros said simply.

"I'll tell her. I know she will be pleased."

After ending the call, Alexandros set the phone on his desk and turned back to the view. The city sprawled beneath him, humming with life. But it felt hollow. Detached.

He closed his eyes and pictured Dani—barefoot on the dock, her skirt dancing in the breeze, that quicksilver smile lighting up her face.

I gave you last night, Dani.

Tonight, Dani, you'll be mine. And this time... you won't want to go.

His jaw tightened with anticipation.

CHAPTER 8

$\mathcal{A}$ dull throb pulsed behind Dani's eyes as she drifted toward consciousness. Her head felt like it was packed with fog—heavy and slow—her limbs numb and awkward.

She blinked once. Twice. Shadows wavered, refusing to take shape.

A sour, metallic tang coated her tongue. Her body felt unmoored—half dream, half nightmare.

She tried to move—and couldn't.

Panic surged.

Her mouth was sealed with thick tape, and her arms were wrenched behind her, bound tightly to something cold and unyielding. A metal pipe. Her legs were curled under her on what felt like an old mattress reeking of mold and sweat. The air was stale, laced with dust and oil. Her breath came in short, sharp bursts through her nose.

She twisted, wincing at the sharp bite of plastic cutting into her skin, until she sat upright.

A wave of dizziness rolled over her.

She leaned her head against the wall, her eyes shut tight, trying not to throw up. Slowly, fragments of memory began to surface.

The phone call with her grandfather.

Her laughter. Her smile. Telling her grandfather about Alexandros.

That warm, floating feeling in her chest as she walked back to the trawler...

Her pulse sped as she remembered. Her heart beat so fast she was afraid she would pass out again.

The shadow.

The voice.

Her eyes flew open, and her body went rigid.

No. No, it can't be.

But it was.

Zayan.

Her breath caught in her throat. She began to tremble uncontrollably.

After all these years... Why?

Her body tensed as her senses, heightened by her fear, picked up the sound of footsteps.

Light. Unhurried. Approaching.

She recoiled as far as she could into the corner, pulling her knees to her chest, trying to make herself small, invisible, anything.

The door creaked open.

Her heart pounded like a war drum.

A man stepped inside. Masked. Tall. His skin was a deep bronze, sun-darkened, but his build—lean, hard—was unmistakable. Scars marked the backs of his hands, jagged white reminders of cruelty lived and dealt.

He carried a stained paper plate with a sandwich and a lukewarm bottle of water. As if that could pass for kindness.

Dani's throat moved in a dry swallow. The ache of thirst burned her. But her fear outweighed everything else.

He crouched, placing the food beside her.

He reached out a dirty hand.

She flinched violently, turning her face away, her heart in her throat.

A low chuckle escaped him—amused, unhurried. Cold.

He grabbed her hair, yanking her head forward with a painful jerk. Her scalp burned as she fought not to cry out.

Then came the searing sting as he ripped the tape from her mouth.

Dani gasped, dragging air into her lungs, her skin raw where the adhesive had torn it. She glared up at him, fury battling terror.

Zayan made a soft tsk, dragging the pad of his rough thumb across her lips with grotesque familiarity. Her stomach lurched with revulsion.

He rose slowly to his full height and turned as if to leave.

"I can't eat like this," Dani rasped, her voice hoarse, raw. "My hands..."

He paused.

Her hope shattered the moment his head snapped back around.

The blow came without warning.

His hand cracked across her face, whipping her head sideways into the metal pipe. Stars exploded in her vision. Pain radiated from her jaw as the coppery tang of blood filled her mouth. Her lip split.

She was still reeling when he grabbed her hair again, yanking her head back at a punishing angle.

From his belt, he drew a fishing knife—long, curved, razor-sharp.

Her breath froze.

She locked eyes with him, refusing to look away, even as the blade sliced through the strap binding her to the pipe. Her arms fell forward, aching and trembling.

He shoved her backward.

Before she could recover, he pulled a new strap from his pocket and fastened one wrist back to the pipe, yanking it tight. Too tight. The plastic dug into her skin.

He straightened and turned to leave.

"Why?" she whispered.

He paused at the door, half in shadow, and looked over his shoulder. His voice was soft. Almost casual.

"Because I can."

And just like that, the nightmare she thought she'd outrun came roaring back.

She flinched when the door slammed shut. Her throat worked up and down as she fought back the paralyzing fear when the lock clicked.

Dani stayed frozen for what felt like hours, her breath ragged, her pulse thundering in her ears. Her cheek throbbed. The skin on her wrist was already raw beneath the strap. The taste of blood in her mouth made her sick to her stomach.

She reached up and touched her face, her fingers trembling.

He's real. This is real.

She shut her eyes, willing herself not to sink into the gnawing dark.

Think. Think, Dani.

She patted her skirt pocket with trembling fingers.

Gone. Her phone—gone. But—

Tears stung her eyes, but she refused to let them fall as she ran her hand down along her right leg to her ankle. Her ankle bracelets were still there. Her fingers trembled as she felt along the beads before caressing the cylinder-shaped metal one.

Thank you, Gramps.

Her gaze shifted to the paper plate beside her. She ignored the sandwich—her stomach twisted at the thought—but reached for the water. She drained half the bottle in desperate gulps before capping it again.

Focus. Breathe.

The room looked as if it had been converted into a storage closet at some point. The air was damp. The walls were grimy. A single dirty window sat high above her, covered in a thin wire and too small to escape through. Still, she stared at it, willing a plan to form.

Her wrist ached where the strap dug in. She twisted slightly, shifting the pressure, testing the give in the pipe behind her.

It groaned faintly. But not enough.

She closed her eyes and sent a silent message—first to her grandfather.

I love you, Gramps. Please don't worry. I won't give up.

And then to Alexandros.

I should have stayed. I wanted to. I was just scared...

A tear slipped down her cheek.

Please. Help me find a way out of here. Please... let me live.

Because Zayan wouldn't let her go—not this time.

She knew it.

His eyes...

It had been impossible to miss his intentions. Her grandfather always said eyes were the windows to a soul.

Zayan's were empty.

Dead.

Because he had no soul left.

LEGAL JARGON BUZZED in the boardroom, as lifeless as the marble table it echoed from.

"...and as for Clause 14.7, we'll need to renegotiate the force majeure protections before final sign—"

Alexandros barely lifted his gaze from the contract in front of him when the door opened. It was only when he caught a flicker of movement—swift, purposeful—that his eyes darted up.

Demetrius.

His head of security rarely entered a closed meeting unless something was wrong.

And something was definitely wrong.

Demetrius's face was pale, drawn, his mouth a grim line as he rounded the table and bent low. The whisper was sharp and clipped, but urgent enough to send a cold spike down Alexandros's spine.

"I need a word. Privately. Now."

Without hesitation, Alexandros rose to his feet. "Ladies. Gentlemen. I'll return shortly."

He crossed the room with the coiled precision of a panther sensing danger. He was almost at the door when the phone in his pocket buzzed. He reached for it instinctively—but Demetrius moved first.

The bodyguard stepped in front of him, hand raised.

Unthinkable.

Demetrius never blocked him. Ever.

"Don't answer it yet," Demetrius said, his voice low as he turned the screen toward Alexandros.

The name on the screen punched the air from his lungs.

Dani.

He answered instantly. "Danika *mou*," he murmured, his voice softening despite the tension thrumming beneath it, his eyes locked on Demetrius's face. "I was just thinking—"

"Alexandros..."

Her voice trembled. Fractured. Not the woman who had defied a yacht full of strangers or laughed at the stars.

The color drained from his face.

"What's wrong?" he demanded.

A scribbled note appeared in front of him, shoved into his hand by Demetrius. His eyes scanned it—once, twice—trying to comprehend the impossible words:

She's been taken. Keep her talking. We're trying to trace the call.

Demetrius was already on his second phone, barking into it in rapid Greek, moving toward the hallway as a second team mobilized behind the scenes.

Alexandros gripped his phone tighter. "Dani, listen to me. Where are you? Are you hurt?"

She didn't respond.

There was a sudden cry of pain—hers—a raw, wrenching sound that stabbed straight through him.

"Dani!"

A male voice cut in. Cold. Cruel. Almost amused.

"If you want your precious girlfriend back in one piece, Kallistratos, I suggest you do exactly as I instructed in the note I'm sure you've found by now. Unless, of course, you'd prefer her returned piece by piece."

A cold sweat broke out across Alexandros's neck.

"You touch her again, and I swear—"

The line went dead.

Silence.

No click. No breath. Just the cold finality of disconnection.

He stood frozen in place, the phone still pressed to his ear, his blood thundering in his skull. The silence rang louder than the threat.

He couldn't breathe. Couldn't think—

Only feel.

And what he felt was rage.

He stared at Demetrius as if the man might somehow undo what had just happened.

She's gone," Alexandros rasped. "He cut the line."

Demetrius swore viciously. "The signal was too short. We couldn't triangulate a location in time. And her phone—whoever has it— they've already shut it down."

Alexandros's jaw clenched. A storm began to build behind his eyes. Fury. Fear. The kind that made men dangerous.

He turned on his heel. "My office. Now."

He passed Julius in the hall without slowing. "Clear my entire schedule. Call Theo. Tell him I need him. Urgently."

"Sir?"

"Tell him to bring his friends—the ones from special operations," Alexandros instructed in a voice devoid of emotion.

He strode into his private office, the door slamming shut behind Demetrius. The floor-to-ceiling windows cast long shadows as the early afternoon sun glinted off steel and glass. But Alexandros felt none of it.

He was cold—colder than he had ever been.

"Tell me everything," he said.

Demetrius didn't waste a second. He handed over a folded note.

A smear of blood marred the edge.

Alexandros stared at it, his throat tightening. "Is it hers?"

"No," Demetrius said. "It's the security guard's. The one watching her. He was attacked last night—bludgeoned, tied up. He was found an hour ago by a friend of Dani's. A guy named Carlos. Carlos said she never showed up for work."

Alexandros unfolded the note with hands that trembled only slightly.

Fifty million euros. Waterproof bag. Coordinates enclosed. No cops. Or I send her back to you in pieces. Start with her beautiful green eyes? Or would you like the ankle with the little beads around it?

He swallowed. Hard. The letters swam in front of him. "How did he get on board?"

"Busted hatch on the trawler. Lock forced. We found signs of a struggle inside the salon." Demetrius's voice was tight. Controlled. "The bastard planned this. Knew where she'd be. How to get in and out. Fast. That she was being watched by security."

"Cameras?"

"Disabled."

Alexandros's eyes burned with fury.

"The police?"

Demetrius pointed to the note. "He said we're free to call them. He'd be 'happy to send body parts' if we did."

Alexandros's gaze locked on the coordinates.

"International waters."

Demetrius nodded grimly. "International waters."

Alexandros's voice turned to granite.

"Then we don't need jurisdiction."

He strode to his desk, pulled open a drawer, and slammed his hand down on a hidden biometric scanner. The small panel beeped, unlocked, and opened to reveal a satellite phone, an encrypted tablet —and something darker, colder.

He looked up.

"Get me eyes on those coordinates," he ordered. "Deploy drones. Activate whatever favors we're owed."

"And the money?"

Alexandros's mouth curled. "He'll get his money, but he won't live to enjoy it."

His gaze dropped to the blood-streaked note again, then turned to the window.

"She's special, Demetrius," he said quietly. His voice cracked, just once. "And this happened to her... because of me."

85

CHAPTER 9

The elevator doors slid open with a chime, but no one in the executive suite looked up. Alexandros's office had become a full-blown command center, humming with urgency and focused chaos.

LED monitors lined one wall, maps flickering in real-time, live feeds streaming, data updating second by second. The once pristine glass-and-steel space was a nest of cables, blinking laptops, and determined voices speaking in hushed, rapid tones.

Theo stepped inside, flanked by two men with close-cropped hair and military bearing. Nikos and Markos peeled off to the perimeter, eyes already scanning the layout and assessing the scene.

Four more were on the way.

This wasn't a rescue mission—it was a declaration of war.

And it was personal.

He locked eyes with Demetrius first and gave a curt nod. The security chief's expression was tight, his jaw clenched like a man barely holding it together.

Alexandros stood at the head of the room, his shoulders rigid, his back to the massive windows. There was something different in his posture. In his eyes.

Theo had seen a lot of men under pressure. But the look on his brother's face chilled him more than any battlefield.

Controlled. Coiled.

Deadly.

The bastard who took Dani has no idea what he's unleashed.

"Alexandros," Theo said, crossing the room.

"Theo." Alexandros gripped his hand, then stepped back. "Thanks for coming."

Theo didn't need thanks. Not for this. "Tell me everything."

Demetrius jumped in, already handing over a map layered with notes and photos. "Dani's trawler. Taken sometime between 11 p.m. and 3 a.m. Forced entry through a hatch. Signs of a struggle inside. The security guard assigned to her was attacked—bludgeoned and tied up. Discovered this morning by a friend of hers, Carlos."

Theo's jaw flexed as he scanned the photos. Rope burns. Blood. A bloody wrench.

He pointed. "Water or land?"

"That's the problem," Demetrius said. "We don't know. Her trawler's moored here—" he pointed "—but the area backs up to a service road. If they went by water, they could've disappeared before anyone noticed. If they went by land, they had a hundred escape routes."

Theo's voice was clipped. "Any cameras?"

"Disabled. Power cut to the dock lights too."

"And communication from the kidnappers?"

Alexandros's voice was low. "Only one, only once. They used Dani's phone to call me. Threatened to send her back in pieces if I didn't deliver fifty million euros. Location drop is offshore. International waters."

Theo's eyes narrowed. "Someone who is familiar with being on the water. And since then?"

"Nothing."

A weighted silence fell over the room.

Theo felt it. That sickening quiet between storms.

The type of silence that turned men into monsters or heroes.

Then—Alexandros's phone rang.

Everyone froze.

Theo stepped closer to look over Alexandros's shoulder.

Unknown number.

Alexandros answered on the third ring with lethal calm. "Kallistratos."

Demetrius handed him an earpiece connected to Alexandros's phone so they could all listen in to the call. What came through the line was not what Theo expected.

"Took you long enough," barked a gruff American voice. "You don't keep an old man waiting. I'm Stuart. Dani's grandfather. Where's my granddaughter? I know she was with you last night, but she's not answering her phone this morning."

Theo blinked. So, Dani was American. That explained the fire in the old man's voice.

Alexandros straightened. "Mr.—Stuart. Dani... she's been taken. She was kidnapped last night off her trawler after I left."

The room stilled again.

Alexandros's voice cracked—just slightly—when he said her name.

And Theo felt it like a blow to the gut. The moment his brother's heart slipped further from his chest.

There was a long beat of silence on the other end of the line.

Theo stiffened when Stuart spoke again. "Dani wears a tracker—hidden in jewelry. She can activate it manually. The battery lasts twenty-four hours tops."

Theo surged forward. "Can he access it?"

Alexandros put the call on speaker. "Stuart, can you access it?"

"One moment. Let me check... Hang on..."

Theo paced like a lion in a cage, every muscle taut, eyes glued to his brother's face. Each second crawled.

The entire room waited with bated breath. Monitors flickered as the tension thickened.

A minute passed before—

"I've got it," Stuart said, his voice coming fast now. "She triggered it about thirty minutes ago. I'm sending the data now. Give me a second to patch it through."

One of Demetrius's techs called out. "Signal received. I've got the beacon."

The map on the wall updated in real-time. A pulsing red dot appeared.

Theo leaned in. "That's near the fishing wharf. East side. Warehouses."

Demetrius cursed. "That area's a goddamn labyrinth. Half those buildings haven't been occupied in years. Perfect place to vanish."

Stuart's voice returned. "You tell me—can you handle this, Alexandros? Or do I need to call in favors of my own?"

Theo glanced at his brother.

Saw the fire behind his eyes.

The fury under control.

"No," Alexandros said quietly. "I'll bring her back."

Theo nodded once, solidly. "We'll bring her home."

Stuart exhaled. "Go. I'll be on the first flight out of New York."

The call ended.

Theo turned back to the map, his eyes locked on the pulsing dot. "We're on the clock. That signal could drift—off by a hundred meters. Easily, if it is a civilian tracker. We need to move fast and quietly. If they see us coming before we reach her…"

He didn't finish the sentence.

He didn't have to.

"The rest of the team is assembling downstairs now. I've been keeping them up-to-date," Markos said from the doorway. "We'll be ready to move in ten."

Theo turned to Alexandros. "You stay here. We go in."

Alexandros's glare could've scorched steel.

"She's mine, Theo."

"And that's why you don't go in. You're too close. One mistake—one slip—and she dies. Let us do this."

Alexandros didn't speak. He had to trust Theo. He had no other choice. He drew a shuddering breath and gave Theo a short, sharp nod.

Theo turned back to the room. "I want schematics. Old blueprints. Sewer access. Drone footage—whatever we can get. Demetrius, keep the local authorities out of the area. I don't care what you have to do. Rob a bank if you have to. Just don't let them engage."

"We'll keep the area secure," Demetrius promised.

Demetrius's team scattered into motion.

Organized chaos erupted—calls made, favors called in, routes mapped, equipment loaded. Weapons readied.

Theo moved with a general's purpose. Every clipped command sliced through the tension like a blade.

"We have one focus. We get in. We locate the girl. We neutralize the threat. We bring her home alive."

He looked once more at the red dot.

"I've done missions for kings, generals, and billionaires," he muttered. "But this one… this one matters most."

Hope flickered in his chest—thin, but fierce.

Hold on, Dani, he thought, his jaw tight with determination. *We're coming for you—and hell's coming with us.*

THE PLASTIC STRAP bit deep into Dani's wrist, slick with blood and sweat. She had twisted, tugged, even tried a trick she once saw on social media—wedging the hem of her skirt under the strap and yanking—but the plastic refused to give. Her skin was raw. Her fingers ached. But she kept at it.

Until finally—defeated—she let her head fall back against the wall with a dull thud.

Her breath trembled in and out.

Gripping the bottle of water between her knees, she uncapped it, poured a splash onto her skirt, and used the damp fabric to clean away the blood from her wrist. The cuts stung fiercely—but pain meant she was still here. Still fighting.

Her eyes lifted toward the small window near the ceiling. The angle of the light had changed. How long had it been? Hours?

Too long.

Her bladder ached, but the thought of Zayan returning—touching her, even speaking to her again—froze her in place. She'd rather piss herself than give him that power.

She closed her eyes, her heart twisting as a fresh wave of fear surged through her.

Alexandros must be frantic by now.

She had wanted to sound strong when Zayan had called him. Cool. Calm. Like she had everything under control. But the second she heard Alexandros—his teasing greeting and his warm voice—her confidence had vanished like smoke in the wind.

Tears pooled and slowly ran down her face as she tried to cling to a tiny fracture of hope. She closed her eyes and focused on the image of Alexandros's face. He was worth fighting for. He was her future. She had to stay strong.

Her grandfather's words came back to her: *"When I saw your grand-mother for the first time, I knew I'd never be the same."*

Her chest clenched.

Alexandros...

She had felt the same.

Tears blurred her vision.

If he still wants anything to do with me... a small voice whispered.

But then she laughed—a short, breathless sound.

No, a man who dove off a yacht to chase me isn't the kind to run from danger. He'll still want me. I've got to believe I'll see him and Gramps again. If I get out of this, I'm going to see what we have. It's special.

She tried not to think of her parents. If she did, she knew she would give up. She couldn't go into that dark place again. What she felt for Alexandros was different. What she felt couldn't be like what her parents had.

She breathed, trying to calm the panic rising in her throat. Alexandros wouldn't run from a situation like this. Especially not from some sick, twisted freak like Zayan.

She shifted, and the mattress beneath her crinkled with a hollow, scraping sound. She opened her eyes, and her gaze drifted down, searching for the cause. A flash of something clear and smooth caught her eye.

She used her heel to pull the edge of the mattress back a little farther.

The flash caught again.

Dani froze, her eyes widening with hope.

She leaned forward slowly, peering beneath the edge of the mattress—and there, barely visible, was a jagged shard of glass.

Her pulse kicked like a drumbeat.

Glass. From the window above…

She stretched her fingers, straining, desperate—until her fingertips brushed the edge. Closer. Closer—

Yes!

Carefully, she wrapped the shard in her skirt to dull the edge, twisted her wrist, and began sawing at the strap attached to the pipe.

The sound was almost imperceptible, but her breath came in broken sobs.

Her fingers slipped more than once. Blood coated the glass. The strap stretched, groaned, resisted.

She didn't dare stop.

Minutes passed before the strap loosened, and her arm fell free.

She whimpered, clutching her wrist. Her fingers were numb, tingling with returning sensation.

You don't have time to rest, Dani. Get free! she told herself.

She turned her attention to the strap binding her ankles. Her hands were shaking now, the glass slipping in her slick grip, but she sawed through it, frantic, every second filled with the creeping dread that Zayan might return before she was free.

Snap.

Her ankles separated. She twisted to her knees, her legs weak and trembling, before she pushed up with a grunt until she stood.

The room spun, and she was forced to reach out. She held onto the wall until the world fell back onto its axis.

But she was up.

Still clutching the jagged glass, she stumbled into the far corner, crouched low, pulled her panties down, and relieved herself with a shuddering sigh of relief. The act felt shameful, but also defiant. She yanked her panties back up.

She was still in control. And now, she had a fighting chance. She breathed deeply, remembering all the lessons her grandfather had insisted she do in case something like this ever happened and he wasn't around to help her.

Pulling her skirt up, she ripped a strip from the hem and wound around the base of the glass shard, creating a crude handle. Her fingers throbbed with pain, but she didn't let go.

She wouldn't get a second chance. Her gaze flew to the door.

If he opened it and saw her standing—saw the straps broken—he would attack immediately. If he had a gun, it would be over before she could defend herself. She remembered the strength of his arms when he grabbed her on the trawler. He was stronger than he had been as a boy.

No, the only way she could defeat him was to take him by surprise—and not be afraid to do whatever was necessary for her to survive.

Her head whipped around, her eyes scanning the room for an idea. A plan.

Nothing. Nowhere to hide.

Then—her gaze snapped to the plastic straps.

She slowly walked back to the mattress, her heart hammering. Every cell in her body rebelled at the idea of sitting back down, pretending to be defenseless again. The terror was so strong she wasn't sure she could do it. She wanted to throw up.

"You can do this," she whispered fiercely, willing her body to obey. "You have to."

She twisted until she was sitting back down where she had been before. With quivering fingers, she picked up the broken ankle strap and placed it back over her ankles as if it had never been cut. Once satisfied Zayan wouldn't be able to tell it had been sliced unless he

S.E. SMITH

really looked, she fumbled to slide her raw, bleeding wrist back through the one still hanging from the pipe.

It hung too loosely—but maybe it would be enough to trick him.

The sound of footsteps coming down the corridor made her heart hammer in her chest. She tucked the glass shard under her skirt, hidden in the folds.

Her lungs burned as she waited.

"Please, give me strength. Please let me get away from him," she whispered, bowing her head and trying to control her breathing.

The footsteps stopped.

Her shivering increased as the click of the lock echoed through her head. She bit her sore lip, watching with growing anxiety as the doorknob turned.

The door creaked.

She dropped her head, letting her hair fall forward over her face.

He took another step toward her, slow and deliberate. The floor creaked beneath his feet.

She didn't want to look up, but she did.

Zayan.

This time, he wasn't wearing a mask.

She felt his eyes on her—hungry, cruel.

"Now," he murmured, his voice thick with malice, "Now we finish what you denied me four years ago, my sweet, Dani."

Paralyzed by fear, her whole body shook, a silent scream trapped in her throat.

"It's time to pay up."

He stepped closer. Her heart beat so loud she was afraid he could hear it.

"What? Nothing to say? You had plenty to say the last time we were together. You said so much that I was run out of Morocco! Each port, your poor, pitiful cries of how I would fleece unsuspecting young tourists out of their innocence and their families out of their money bit at my heels until I could find no one to seduce. I had to work—*work like a dog*—in low-paying jobs that took my looks from me! But, now... now, it is time to repay me for what you have taken.

I'll take everything from you—your body, your boyfriend's money, your beauty. Then, it will be women like you who will try to seduce me instead, yes?"

He reached out to caress her bruised cheek. He chuckled when she jerked her head back. Her eyes flashed a warning for him to keep his hands off her.

"But, I'm sure by now... you're not so innocent anymore." His voice turned mocking. "Such a shame. I could have been your first." He leaned forward, his putrid breath making her want to gag, and whispered in her ear. "But, I promise I will be your last."

"Go to hell," she whispered, her hand tightening on her makeshift knife as he straightened.

She swallowed when he reached down, gripped the hem of his shirt and pulled it over his head.

Her stomach churned.

He wasn't going to let her leave—no matter what Alexandros paid. She knew it now, with a certainty that chilled her soul.

Her fingers tightened around the glass, the ragged edge digging into her palm.

The scream built in her throat.

She didn't dare let it out.

Not yet.

Not until the right moment.

Zayan was three steps away when he froze, staring at the wall above her head. She looked up, seeing what he saw. A perfect, bloody handprint. A frown creased his face.

His gaze narrowed. A flicker of suspicion. Too late.

She knew that her time was up when his gaze slowly turned towards her.

Bruised. Bloodied. But not broken—

Dani surged up like a demon from hell.

CHAPTER 10

*T*he glass trembled in Alexandros's hand, ice clinking against the crystal.

He didn't blink—just stared—then slowly set it on the tray beside the conference room's minibar.

Bourbon. Untasted. He'd poured it out of habit, like a man acting on muscle memory.

His hand trembled, betraying the turmoil threatening to crush him.

He curled fingers into a fist—his knuckles whitening, his skin stretched tight. It didn't help. Not really.

The sleek conference room—once a cradle of billion-euro deals—felt sterile. Cold.

The overhead lights hummed, their glow too sharp, too precise. It wasn't a sanctuary anymore. It was a cage.

Behind the frosted glass walls, the command center buzzed like a hive—Demetrius had stayed behind to coordinate the ground teams. Drones hovered overhead. His brother's team and private security were on the move. Theo's voice crackled through the comms—calm, lethal, precise. A soldier's voice.

Alexandros sat at the long table alone.

Utterly helpless...

So... powerless.

His palms pressed flat against the polished wood as he leaned forward, his head bowed—his muscles straining to contain the storm rising inside.

Guilt was a cruel beast—relentless, gnawing, whispering insidious doubts in his head.

This is your fault. She trusted you. You were supposed to protect her.

He squeezed his eyes shut.

The image of Dani's beautiful, smiling face haunted him. Yet, it was the sound of her voice on the call—quivering, brave, terrified—that echoed in his head.

Theo would bring her back. He had to.

And when he did... Alexandros would do the only thing left he could do to keep her safe.

He would send her away—to protect her from the danger he'd brought to her door.

It would tear him in half.

But he'd survive. Because she would.

He didn't deserve her. Not if loving him put her in a monster's crosshairs.

The conference room's speakers hummed to life, and his head lifted. His eyes fixed on the dots moving across the screen mounted on the wall.

"Team Alpha, in position."

The voice of Demetrius's team lead came through, clipped and focused.

"Drone confirms the beacon is coming from Warehouse 14. Two-story structure. Satellite shows partial roof collapse. Minimal exterior lighting. We've got one heat signature—possibly two."

"Understood," Theo's voice replied. Calm. Steady. Cold as a scalpel. "Markos, Nikos, north entrance. Luke, Sebastian, take the west. Angel, Cole, do you have eyes up high?"

"Roger that," Angel said.

"Moving into position now," Cole said.

Theo's voice rang through again. "I'm taking the east entrance. Move in."

"Copy."

"Demetrius, confirm exit routes are secure."

"Exits are secure. Three teams have the surrounding area blocked off. We have cooperation from the local authorities. They are on standby if we need them."

Alexandros's fingers clenched on the armrest of his chair.

He pictured the building. Dani trapped inside. Her attacker somewhere near her.

God!

He pushed to his feet, pacing to the far end of the room, but the walls closed in. He felt like he was about to go mad. He had never felt so helpless. So… useless. He knew that every second counted.

He stiffened when a beat of silence came across the feed.

Theo spoke again: "Move in on my mark."

Alexandros stopped breathing.

The silence on the line was deafening.

"Mark."

Static crackled.

Muffled footfalls.

The low, metallic clicks of the weapons' safeties being released echoed in the tense silence.

A door creaked open.

Glass crunched under boots.

Theo's voice was low. "Moving in. It's dark. Smells like oil and mold. Be advised—there's fresh blood on the floor."

A growl tore through Alexandros's throat.

He wanted to rip through the walls. To storm the warehouse himself. To pull her from that hell and carry her home. Instead, he watched the live feed coming in from the front of the half-dozen men scouring the warehouse.

Theo swept the area, moving in a slow, steady, graceful movement that spoke of his years in Special Ops.

Theo swung around, his weapon at the ready.

A sound. Muffled. Desperate.

"Movement. First floor. East corner," one of the team whispered. "I see her—damn, she's running!"

Alexandros's heart exploded in his chest.

Theo's voice surged. "Dani! Hold your ground!"

Another voice. A scream. Hers.

"Alexandros! Alexandros, help me!"

Gunfire erupted. Shouts followed. Glass shattered. Boots slammed against metal stairs.

Theo called out, "I've got her! I've got her!"

Alexandros sank into the chair, his hand trembling over his mouth as Dani's sobs tore through the feed. The body cam caught the blood on her face, her clothes.

"Alexandros—he said... he said he came back—please! Don't let him get me again. Please, Alexandros—"

"You're safe," Theo said, his voice a soothing anchor. "I've got you. You're going home. He'll never touch you again."

Alexandros's chest heaved. He pressed a hand against it like he could hold his heart together.

"I want Alexandros—" Dani gasped through tears. "I want him—please—take me to him."

"You will see him. I promise. You're safe. Alexandros is waiting. Just hold on."

A sob burst from her so raw it split Alexandros open.

Alexandros stiffened when he heard the change in Theo's voice.

It was sharper—tense.

"We need a medic. Stat!"

Alexandros froze.

No!

More static. A garbled response.

In the background, he could hear sirens blaring, steadily growing louder.

Suddenly, more gunfire erupted. The whump of boots and shouted commands.

The audio feed cut out. Then, the body cam went dead.

The quiet in the room was deafening.

The world tilted.

Alexandros pressed his palms to the table to keep from collapsing. Nausea churned in his stomach. Nothing in his life had prepared him for this-this feeling. This excruciating pain.

The door opened behind him.

He turned, feeling shattered.

His father stood there.

The Kallistratos patriarch. Ramrod straight. Silver at his temples. Power emanated from him like Zeus ready to strike.

"I heard," Christos said, his voice like gravel. "They're taking her to the hospital."

Alexandros couldn't speak. He could only nod.

Christos's gaze softened—just a breath. Just enough.

"Come," he said. "We go now. Theo will meet us there."

Alexandros moved.

No hesitation.

He would be at Dani's side when she opened her eyes.

And nothing—not her trauma, not his guilt, not even the demons he would carry forever—would take her from him again.

Not until I know she's safe, he thought grimly.

DANI SUCKED IN A TERRIFIED BREATH. Her eyes met Zayan's, and in that instant, Zayan knew—she was free. As he reached for her, Dani, fueled by adrenaline and fear, surged upward with a desperate lunge.

The shard of glass she'd hidden under her skirt flashed in her hand as she drove it into his side.

His roar of pain and rage was deafening.

He stumbled, then collapsed on top of her, knocking the breath from her lungs. His weight pressed her into the mattress, his hands scrabbling for control. Her muscles burned as they struggled. She thrashed beneath him, clawing, twisting, fighting with every ounce of fury she had.

She cried out when his fingers sank into her raw flesh.

Pain exploded through her arm as he slammed her wrist against the rusted pipe.

Her makeshift blade clattered to the floor.

"No!" she choked out.

But she wasn't done. Jerking her head forward, she smashed her forehead into his nose. Stars danced in front of her eyes from the blow, but she wasn't going to go down without a fight.

She brought her knee up, striking him hard—once, twice—before he grunted in fury and released her. She wrenched sideways, slipping from beneath him just as he reached for her ankle.

His fingers brushed her skin.

She kicked out—connecting with the raw wound where she'd stabbed him.

Zayan released a guttural scream. "You little bitch!"

Dani scrambled to her feet and lunged for the door. Her blood-slick fingers fumbled with the doorknob, finally wrenching it open. She burst into the hallway—blinded briefly by the bright light before she turned and ran.

She didn't know where she was going. Her bare feet slapped against the concrete as she tore through the corridor. She needed an exit. A sign, anything.

"Dani!" Zayan's voice thundered behind her.

A gunshot rang out.

She flinched, veering left. A second shot cracked past her head.

Something burned—a fiery sting across her upper arm. She cried out, stumbling sideways, her shoulder slamming into the wall. She crumpled to her knees.

But she didn't stop.

A sob burst from her chest as she forced herself up, her breath ragged, blood dripping from her arm.

Keep going. Keep going. He can hurt you only if you stop.

She spotted a metal staircase and ran for it.

Another shot exploded behind her. A chunk of the wall burst near her head.

"Run all you want," Zayan roared. "There's nowhere left to hide!"

She stumbled down the stairs two at a time, the world tilting, her vision tunneling from blood loss and fear. The warehouse came into view—open, industrial, shadows moving.

And then—

A door.

Open, glowing with sunlight.

Freedom.

She bolted toward it.

She was ten feet away when a hand grabbed her.

She screamed—raw, terrified, wild.

"No! Let me go!" she shrieked, twisting, striking out.

But the voice that caught her froze her in place.

"I've got you! Dani, it's okay. I've got you."

She blinked up through a haze of panic, her heart slamming against her ribs.

Dark eyes. Familiar. Fierce. Gentle.

"Alexandros?" she gasped.

"No. Theo. I'm his brother," he said, steady and calm. "You're safe now. I promise."

She collapsed against him, her legs buckling, relief and pain crashing over her like a tidal wave.

Theo wrapped an arm around her, dragging her down with him behind a column of crates. He spoke into his comms, his voice terse. "I've got her. She's alive, but bleeding. We need a medic, stat!"

Gunfire erupted nearby. Boots pounded against the floor.

Dani clung to him, sobbing, unable to stop. "He said he came back... I thought he would kill me... I didn't know where to go... I wanted—I needed—Alexandros—"

Theo's voice didn't waver. "I know. He's waiting for you. You're going home."

"I want him," she whispered. "Please, I want him."

"You'll see him soon. Just stay with me, alright? I've got you."

She nodded against his chest, her body shaking uncontrollably.

More shouting echoed through the warehouse. The sound of a

second gun battle broke out. Additional sirens wailed in the distance. Theo's voice barked orders into the comms.

Dani's world tilted again.

Everything hurt. Blood trailed down her arm. Her body was battered—bruises, cuts, gunshot—but something inside her had survived. She wasn't broken. Not anymore.

She was free.

She was safe.

Most of all, she was going home.

Her eyes, weighted with fatigue, finally closed. She released a soft breath. It wasn't fear that claimed her—but fragile peace... and the promise of seeing Alexandros again.

CHAPTER 11

The rhythmic beeping of the heart monitor was the only sound—steady, soothing in its constancy.

The private hospital suite was dimly lit, the overhead lights turned off hours ago. A single lamp cast a warm, yellowish-sheen over the room, pooling across the pale linen sheets and Dani's bruised, sleeping form. Shadows stretched across the whitewashed walls. Beyond the window, city lights flickered like distant stars, their colors dancing faintly on the polished floor tiles.

Alexandros sat in the corner chair, still dressed in the same black slacks and white dress shirt from earlier, now rumpled and wrinkled. His jacket was folded neatly over the armrest. His feet flat against the floor. He cradled a now-cold cup of coffee, untouched. Elbows braced on his knees, his shoulders curled in quiet vigilance. He had barely moved since Dani had been transferred here from downstairs.

She lay motionless in the hospital bed, a thin white blanket pulled to her chest. Her arm—wrapped in a fresh bandage—rested lightly across her stomach. A bruise had bloomed high on her cheekbone, another near her collarbone. Cuts, scrapes, and pain painted her skin like a canvas of survival. And yet—her expression was peaceful. At last.

They'd sedated her after she woke up screaming. Twice.

He hadn't left her side. He couldn't.

A gentle knock sounded at the door.

Alexandros turned his head slightly as the door cracked open. Theo's face appeared in the sliver of space, his dark gaze searching the room.

Alexandros gave a brief nod.

Theo stepped inside, quietly easing the door shut behind him. He looked at Dani, his jaw tightening at the sight of her injuries. Without a word, he pulled over a second chair and sank into it beside his brother.

"Will we wake her if we talk?" Theo asked in a low voice.

Alexandros shook his head. "No. They gave her something to help her rest."

Theo nodded, exhaling quietly.

For a moment, they both stared at Dani. The silence between them was not uncomfortable—just heavy, like air thickened with everything they hadn't said yet.

Alexandros finally broke it.

"Did you get him?"

Theo nodded slowly. "Yeah. But identifying him... that's been tricky."

Alexandros turned to him, his brow furrowed.

Theo continued, "He didn't have any real identification on him. No digital footprint, nothing we can trace. Authorities think he used aliases. But it's been turned over to them now. The man was killed after he opened fire on our team."

Alexandros exhaled—not in relief, but in bitter surrender.

Still, it wasn't enough. Nothing would be.

"This is my fault," he murmured, staring at his hands. "If it weren't for me, she never would've been taken."

Theo frowned. "What are you talking about?"

"She was targeted because of us. Because of me. Because of the money. The name. If I'd protected her properly, she never would've—"

"That's not true."

The voice was quiet. Steady. And came from the doorway.

Both men turned.

An older man with thick gray hair stood there, framed in the soft light spilling from the hallway. His navy-blue sweater was worn, his khakis rumpled, his expression carved from granite and sorrow. But his eyes were clear. Focused.

Alexandros and Theo rose immediately, instinctively. He recognized the man's voice as Stuart, Dani's grandfather.

Stuart walked over to the bed, his movements slow but steady. He bent over Dani, his hand brushing her curls back from her forehead with the tenderness of a man who had been a part of her life since infancy. He pressed a kiss to her brow, closed his eyes for a long moment, then exhaled deeply.

"I love you, girl. You did good. You did real good," Stuart murmured with a sigh.

When he straightened, he looked at them both with quiet gravity.

"Come," he said, his voice low. "Let's go down to the cafeteria. We could all use some coffee."

Alexandros hesitated. His gaze dropped back to Dani.

Stuart placed a gentle hand on his shoulder. "She's safe now, son. And there's something I think you need to know. It might help ease some of the guilt I can see on your face."

His words hung in the air like a thread about to unravel everything.

Alexandros exchanged a glance with Theo.

Then, with a torn glance at Dani, he followed Stuart into the hall.

"I'm surprised you made it from New York to Athens so fast," Theo said as the elevator descended.

Stuart gave a tired chuckle. "It helps when you have the resources. I've never formally introduced myself. My name is Stuart Bouras."

"Bouras? As in *the* Stuart Bouras of *Bouras International*?" Alexandros asked, his voice coming out on a hiss of disbelief.

"The one and only," Stuart replied with a faint smile.

"*Tee sto gha-MO-to?!*" What the hell?! Theo muttered, staring back and forth between Stuart and Alexandros. "I thought you said Dani was a mechanic."

Stuart chuckled again and nodded. "Let's get the coffee, and I'll explain."

Several minutes later, Alexandros sat with his back against the wall at a corner table in the cafeteria, waiting as his brother and Stuart finished ordering a meal. His mind was shattered, trying to connect how Dani, his barefoot mermaid who cooed to her leather tool bag, was in reality the granddaughter of one of the wealthiest men in the world. Even wealthier than he was!

Bouras International wasn't just powerful—it was a trillion-dollar behemoth. How the hell had Stuart allowed his only heir to live unprotected on a rusting trawler, working as a marine mechanic?

Anger churned inside him, hot and sharp. The more he thought about the dangers Dani must've faced, the tighter his chest became.

"Take your blood pressure down a notch, son," Stuart said, sliding into the chair across from him.

"How could you allow her to be in this kind of danger?" he demanded, sitting back.

He knew his brown eyes were spitting fire. He didn't care. Even he and Theo—who had spent years in Special Operations—kept a security detail on standby. That was why Theo had two of his team with him before he even made the call.

Stuart shook his head. "Dani had security. It didn't mean that she *knew* she had security, but she had it." He nodded at him. "Carlos, the man who found your guy, is one of them. Maria, is another. She is acting as Carlos's girlfriend. I knew you had a guy watching over Dani, so I told Carlos to pull back so it wouldn't cause trouble. That was my mistake."

"The man who-who kidnapped Dani—," Alexandros started.

"His name is Zayan Alaoui—or it was four years ago," Stuart said, his voice dropping deeper with regret.

"You know who he is?" Theo demanded.

S.E. SMITH

Stuart nodded, wrapping his hands around his coffee cup and releasing a deep sigh. He stared down at his uneaten food before he pushed it away, sat back, and studied Alexandros.

"Has Dani told you anything about her past?" Stuart suddenly asked.

Alexandros frowned. "Not much. She just told me that her parents died in a small plane crash when she was fifteen."

Stuart sat forward, resting his elbows on the table. "You must mean something to her if she told you that much. She doesn't talk about it—ever. Not to me. Not to the therapist I hired."

"What does this have to do with Zayan Alaoui?" Theo asked with a frown.

"After the accident, Dani withdrew deep into herself. She barely talked. For almost a year, she just stared into space. It was as if she had lost all desire to live. It scared the hell out of me. No one could get through the walls she had erected." Moisture glazed Stuart's eyes before he blinked them away. "As a last resort, I packed Dani up and we took off with no destination in mind. We spent time in Ireland, hiking in the highlands. Spent a month in England before we decided we didn't like the food. Took the train to France—where we liked the food a little too much." Alexandros's lips twitched when Stuart patted his belly and smiled.

"Did that help her?" Alexandros asked in a quiet voice.

Stuart sniffed and rubbed his hand under his nose. "Yeah. She slowly began to blossom. It didn't happen overnight, but I could see the change. She really opened up when we made it to Italy. One day we were down at the docks. We were just going to watch the sunset. As we were sitting there, we were watching a fisherman on this old fishing trawler. He was working on the engine and cussing up a storm. Out of the blue, Dani stands up, walks over to him, and asks if she can help him. I don't know who was more shocked, me or that damn Italian!"

Stuart chuckled, sniffed, and wiped a dot of moisture from the corner of his eye. Alexandros could *feel* the emotion vibrating within the older man. In his mind's eye, he was picturing a very young, shattered Dani, reaching out, a wrench in her hand, a smidge of grease across her cheek, her beautiful auburn hair piled in a messy bun and held in place by a colorful scarf.

I'm falling for her. No—I'm already gone. I am in love with her.

The realization struck him like one of Zeus's lightning rods. He swallowed, pushing his new discovery into a corner of his mind until he could unpackage it later—when he was alone.

"I'm still waiting for the Alaoui connection," Theo said.

Stuart snorted and looked at Theo with amusement. "Impatient, are you? You did good, going in after Dani. That was some Class A military maneuver."

"Thank you," Theo responded in a dry tone. "Alaoui?"

"Shortened version, I bought the trawler from the fisherman who was more than happy to sell it for a profit, Dani and I fixed it up, and we decided we'd do a bit more exploring. We ended up in Morocco. Zayan was a dock rat. He made his living off of finding beautiful young foreign women who were looking for romance or who were vulnerable. He targeted Dani. If they were lucky, Zayan would seduce them with promises of love and adventure while stealing them blind. I found out later that he would also pick certain young women for human trafficking. Dani was marked for that. Her hair and physical beauty made her unique—and valuable," Stuart said in a blunt tone.

Alexandros hissed while Theo cursed under his breath. Horror gripped Alexandros at the thought of what could have happened to Dani. That horror grew when he wondered if Zayan had—

"How old was she?" Alexandros bit out.

"Seventeen. Dani never knew about the other stuff Zayan was involved in. She also didn't know that I had security monitoring the situation. I knew she was vulnerable. And as much as I hated it, I had to give her space. The report I received said that Dani caught Zayan working his charms with other young tourists. Not all of them were women."

"Poor Dani," Theo said with a shake of his head.

Stuart grinned, though the smile didn't reach his eyes. "Don't feel sorry for her. She fought back. By the time she got done with him,

S.E. SMITH

Zayan's little business in that port was finished. By the time I got done with him, he couldn't seduce a chicken. His handlers weren't happy with his performance. After a few encounters with their fists, let's just say he wasn't looking so pretty anymore. Unable to make a living using his looks, he had to start actually working to make a living. Three years ago, he disappeared off the radar."

"Until last night," Alexandros said.

Stuart nodded. "Until last night. As far as my security guys can tell, he must have recognized Dani. If anything, she is more beautiful than she was before. He saw her with you and decided to have his revenge and make some money off of the deal."

"He wasn't going to let her go," Theo said, looking down at the cold, black liquid in his cup before he looked up. "Markos found a room—" He breathed deeply and shook his head, looking down again. "He wasn't going to let her go."

"Thank you both—for saving Dani. I owe you a life debt that I'll never be able to repay," Stuart said, his voice not quite steady.

Emotion swept through him, and he suddenly knew what he needed—no had—to do. This world was too cruel for someone as beautiful as Dani. She needed to be protected, and he would do whatever he had to do to make that happen.

"You can," Alexandros said. "By giving me her hand in marriage."

Theo sputtered. "What?!" He gaped at his brother. "Alexandros—"

"I'll protect her," Alexandros said, eyes locked on Stuart's. "With everything I am. I swear it."

Stuart raised an eyebrow, watching him closely. "You realize Dani's not a porcelain doll. She won't let you lock her in a gilded cage. She'd fight you tooth and nail if you tried."

"I wouldn't expect anything less." His voice turned to steel. "But I'll be damned if anyone ever lays a hand on her again."

CHAPTER 12

a low, familiar voice tugged Dani from the depths of sleep.
It was gravelly and deep, laced with warmth and quiet
strength—the voice that had read her bedtime stories, taught her to tie
knots, and always made her feel safe.

Her lips curved into a weak smile.

Gramps.

She shifted—and pain lanced through her arm, shoulder, and side.

The voice stopped mid-sentence.

"Dani?" Stuart's voice now carried a distinct note—concern, sharp
and immediate.

She forced her eyes open, blinking against the dull light. Her
grandfather was already by her side, sliding his phone into his pocket.
Relief flooded his features when their eyes met.

"There she is. There's my beautiful girl," he said softly, his crooked
smile creasing his weathered face.

Tears welled in her eyes and blurred her vision as she reached out
her good arm toward him.

He didn't hesitate. Stuart leaned over and wrapped his arms gently
around her, mindful of her injuries. His embrace was warm and

familiar, enveloping her like a shield against the nightmare that had almost swallowed her whole.

She inhaled deeply, letting the scent of his aftershave—woodsy and clean—settle over her. He pulled back after a minute, his hand brushing her tangled hair from her face.

"You're here," she whispered, her voice hoarse with emotion.

"Of course I am. Where else would I be?" he murmured, taking her hand and giving it a gentle squeeze.

A watery smile tugged at her lips. "And still a fashion icon, I see. Is that your favorite moth-eaten sweater from the '90s? And a wrinkled shirt you probably yanked from the laundry basket?"

Stuart huffed a laugh and rubbed his nose. "Don't sass your elders when you're busted up in a hospital bed."

Her smile wobbled. "I love you."

He cleared his throat, glanced away, and gave a small sniff. "Love you too, sweetheart. You gave your gramps a bit of a scare this time."

"I'm sorry," she whispered.

He shook his head and sank back into the chair beside her bed, brushing a hand through his graying hair. Dani pressed the controls, lifting the bed slowly into a sitting position. She gritted her teeth as her bruises protested the movement, but she didn't stop.

"Ain't nothing for you to be sorry about, Dani. It was that jackass who took you that's to blame. He'll never hurt you again."

"Thank you," she said quietly, her eyes fixed on his. "For encouraging me to wear the tracker. You were right—like always. It did come in handy."

His expression crumpled at the edges. "Dani…"

Tears slipped down her cheeks, warm and silent. Stuart reached into the side drawer, pulled out a tissue, and handed it to her without a word.

She wiped her eyes and nodded. "What happened?"

He exhaled long and low. "It was Zayan."

She nodded, her breath catching. "Yeah, I know."

"He recognized you; thought he saw an opportunity and took it."

"He wanted revenge," she murmured. "He was going to—."

Her voice faltered. She closed her eyes, breathed, and pushed her fear away. Zayan would never harm her again.

Stuart looked down at his hands before he gazed back at her, his expression grave.

"I should have seen it coming. I knew what he was years ago. I pulled the security back when I shouldn't have. I... I got too comfortable."

"No," she said firmly, reaching for his hand again. Her grip was weak, but her voice wasn't. "Zayan made his own choices. We didn't do this. He did."

His eyes flicked up to hers, moist but grateful.

She gave him a small, tearful smile.

A shift in the air made her glance toward the doorway—and her breath hitched.

Alexandros stood there...

His eyes locked on hers with such intensity, such raw emotion, it made her chest ache.

He looked wrecked—and beautiful. His dark hair was tousled, as if he had been running his fingers through it. His sleeves were rolled to the elbows and the top buttons of his shirt undone. He looked like a man who hadn't slept, hadn't stopped, hadn't breathed until he saw her open her eyes.

Before she could speak, her grandfather abruptly stood and stretched, bones cracking in protest. He yawned dramatically.

"Well," Stuart said, patting his belly. "Next shift's here."

She blinked. "Wait, what—?"

He leaned down, kissed her temple, and whispered, "I'll see you later, honey. Be kind to him."

Then he turned toward Alexandros with a knowing look, murmured, "Good luck," and strolled out like he hadn't just dropped a brick of implication on the room.

The door clicked softly shut behind him.

Dani's gaze flicked back to Alexandros.

He stepped forward, silent, purposeful.

Her heart stuttered as he neared her bed, his eyes never leaving hers.

She sat straighter, suddenly breathless—not from pain this time, but from the heat building in the air between them.

Whatever storm had passed... another was about to begin.

Four weeks.

Twenty-eight days.

Six hundred and seventy-two hours.

...And she was this close to yanking out Alexandros's hair by the roots. Or better yet, her grandfather's. Or both. Possibly at the same time.

Dani sat cross-legged in the warm sand, the sun brushing her skin like a lazy cat. A salty breeze curled around her, teasing the ends of her messy braid and carrying the faint sound of waves kissing the shore. The private beach on Alexandros's family island was paradise—powder-soft sand, a view straight off a postcard, and absolute serenity.

Too much serenity.

She was going stir-crazy.

The villa perched above her like a watchful chaperone, and she swore one of the staff probably had binoculars trained on her right now to report back to the Overprotective Greek Coalition—aka her grandfather and Alexandros.

She dug her toes into the sand and muttered under her breath, "I survived a plane crash, a kidnapping, a stab wound, and a lunatic with a vendetta... only to be smothered by two Greek mother hens the size of marble statues."

She could still hear their voices echoing in her head from the hospital:

"You need to stay one more night."

"The doctor said—"

"Don't argue, *koutaváki mou*, your stitches—"

Ugh. The stitches.

She hadn't even realized she'd been stabbed until the doctor explained they'd had to go in and close the wound properly. Apparently, in the middle of her adrenaline-fueled escape, Zayan had used the knife he had brought to cut the damn straps on her instead.

But that was weeks ago.

The stitches were out. The bruises had faded. She was stronger. Healing.

Physically, anyway.

The nightmares were another story.

But even those, she could've handled—if not for the emotional whiplash of waking up to find Alexandros holding her during the night, only to roll over again in the morning and find nothing but empty sheets. Every. Damn. Time.

She was going to combust.

She wasn't even sure it was sexual frustration anymore—it was existential.

How could one man radiate that much smolder and still refuse to touch her?

Every time he looked at her, it was like she was the center of his universe. His gaze stripped her to the soul. And yet, every time she reached out, he pulled back with that tortured *'I can't risk breaking you'* look.

As if she were made of glass.

Newsflash: she was not.

She snorted, resting her chin on her knees and glaring at the horizon. The trawler bobbed just off the coast; the sun glinting off the rusting metal and peeling paint as if it was winking at her.

She could swim that far. With desperation and frustration on her side, she could swim twice that distance.

Her gaze narrowed.

The urge to flee twisted in her gut like a rip current.

That boat was freedom. No expectations, no wedding talk, no mysterious secret Greek family alliances that suddenly had her grandfather and Alexandros's mother and father chatting about guest lists and floral arrangements like they were co-planning the Royal Wedding.

Eleni had been absolutely glowing ever since Dani arrived. She mothered her like her own, brought her special tea for sleep and sweets for energy, and cooed every time Dani so much as coughed. There were three words to describe Alexandros's mother: Sweet. Endearing.

And terrifying.

Especially when the words "spring wedding" and "off-the-shoulder lace" had floated out of her mouth last night at dinner.

No.

No, no, no.

Did she want to sleep with Eleni and Christos's obscenely sexy youngest son?

Hell yes.

Did she want to marry him?

Hell no.

She was only twenty-one, still trying to figure out who she was without a wrench in her hand or saltwater in her hair. Marriage felt like a chapter she hadn't even read the prologue for yet. Maybe in five or ten years—but not now. Not like this.

She bit her lip, still eyeing the trawler.

Could she do it? Swim out there? Before security caught her? It wasn't that far…

She pictured herself climbing aboard, taking the wheel, disappearing around the bend like a sea ghost.

Just her and the horizon.

No overbearing Greek men. No pressure. No—

With a dramatic groan, she flopped onto the sand like a beached starfish, limbs splayed, dignity optional.

The villa loomed above. The trawler rocked gently offshore.

Stay or run.

Want or need.

Her arms covered her face as she groaned into them. "I am losing my freaking mind."

Because as much as she wanted to run...

As much as she needed to breathe...

She also wanted him.

Alexandros.

And she wasn't sure which would break her first—running from him...

Or staying and never touching him.

THE INDISTINCT MURMUR of voices behind him barely registered. His father and Stuart were deep in discussion—numbers, projections, empire-building. The merger between Kallistratos and Bouras was monumental. The seismic shift that would send tremors through global markets, realign power structures, and make headlines around the world.

Alexandros didn't care.

Not about the company. Not about the legacy. Not about fortune.

Not when she was out there.

He stood at the window of the villa's study, his hands curled in his pockets, his gaze fixed on the woman seated on the sand below. Dani sat cross-legged, her back to the house, a stubborn line to her shoulders as the wind tousled her hair. Her profile was etched against the horizon, silhouetted by the glow of the late afternoon sun.

She was beautiful. Wild. Untamed.

And slipping away from him.

He clenched his jaw, his fingers twitching with the need to touch her.

Every part of him ached with frustration.

He had thought asking Stuart for Dani's hand in marriage was the hard part. He hadn't expected the man to show up uninvited at their family home and announce the news over coffee like it was already done. His mother had immediately lit up like a chandelier, her joy filling the villa, her wedding planner on speed dial before Alexandros could even finish his next breath.

But none of that mattered.

He hadn't asked her yet.

And Dani didn't belong to anyone.

She had remained silent, but he had felt her growing restlessness. She wouldn't accept him—unless she chose to.

And right now, she wasn't choosing him.

Every night since she had come home from the hospital, he had held her.

She hadn't asked. She hadn't needed to.

The first night, her screams ripped through the silence like a blade. Crashing through the connecting doors of the bedrooms, his heart pounding, he'd found her tangled in sweat-soaked sheets, thrashing like a cornered animal. He'd climbed into bed beside her and wrapped her in his arms. Her wild sobs had turned into soft hiccups, her trembling into calm. He had stayed until the sun crept over the horizon, then slipped out before she woke.

It had happened again.

And again.

Until sneaking into her bed became his ritual. His necessity. He held her like a lifeline, but never crossed the invisible line between need and permission. He buried the hunger, the heat. Night after night, he left her untouched—and it was breaking him.

She curled against him like she was home—like she needed him— even so, he didn't touch her the way he dreamed of touching her. He didn't kiss her. He didn't take what his entire body ached for.

He wouldn't—couldn't—until she was ready. At first, it had been because her body needed to heal. Now, it was her mind.

But the past week… The past week was testing every ounce of restraint he had.

There were moments he would wake before her, watching her sleep with one hand tangled in the hair on his chest, her breath feathering across his throat—and it took everything in him not to whisper her name and wake her with a kiss. To cover her body with his and sink into her like a dying man searching for the elixir of life.

Her scent was on his skin. Her warmth had wrapped its way

around his body until he couldn't tell where she began and he ended. They were destined to be one—whether she accepted that truth yet or not.

But what he saw now from the window chilled him more than all the nights after he had left her bed aching.

She stood up.

From his vantage point, he could see her staring at *The Gentle Breeze*—the battered old trawler rocking gently on the turquoise sea. Her trawler. Her escape.

He saw it happen in slow motion—her gaze drifting over the waves, her body leaning forward, drawn like the tide. His gut clenched as she took a single step toward the water. She looked small from this distance, a lone figure poised at the edge of a choice. His fingers tightened around his phone; he was ready to text Demetrius, who he knew was watching the same scene unfold.

Run or stay.

He could feel an invisible pull inside her. The need to flee. To reclaim her sense of self, her freedom. She was a storm caught in a glass bottle, and the pressure was building.

She turned away, just slightly, and his heart stuttered in relief.

But then she stopped again.

Her head tilted. Her shoulders hesitated. It was like some part of her heart was still tangled in the sea, whispering that it wasn't too late. That she could still run before she was shackled. Before her name was printed on wedding invitations she hadn't approved.

He wanted to curse. To shout. To race down to the beach and drag her into his arms.

But he didn't move.

And then—she looked up.

Their eyes met across the distance, a heartbeat suspended in time.

The wind tossed her hair, the light caught her eyes, and Alexandros saw everything in that one glance—her longing, her defiance, her confusion, her need. And buried beneath it all, a question: *Will you come after me, or will you let me go?*

Something inside him snapped.

Not with anger.

Not with lust.

With resolve.

He would not lose her.

He couldn't.

She might think she needed to find herself before she could give herself. But what she didn't understand—what she hadn't yet let herself feel—was that with him, she didn't have to give up anything. He didn't want to tame her. He didn't want to trap her. He just wanted to be the man she could run to—not from.

And tonight, before she vanished like sea foam, he would claim her.

He would go to her, not to hold her like a broken doll, but to love her like a woman who set him on fire every time she breathed.

She was his mermaid.

And tonight, before she slipped through his fingers like sea foam, he would claim her.

Not out of dominance.

Not out of fear.

But because they both needed it.

He turned from the window, fire in his chest and purpose in his steps.

It was time.

CHAPTER 13

*T*he clink of silverware, the hum of polite conversation, Alexandros's father talking business with her grandfather —it all blurred into background noise.

Dani sat stiffly, her nerves stretched taut like rigging on a storm-pulled sail.

She could feel it building.

The pressure.

The urge to move. To do something. Anything. Run. Jump. Scream. Strip him naked and straddle him right there at the table.

It didn't help that Alexandros looked like a Greek god tonight—shirt open at the collar, sleeves rolled to reveal strong, tanned forearms, that maddening aftershave curling around her like a dark, masculine spell. She could feel the buzz of him—his heat, his awareness—tugging at her skin every time he shifted beside her.

She tried to pretend nothing was wrong, but she knew she wasn't that great an actress. Holding her breath, counting to one hundred— heck, even thinking of sheep wasn't working. Her switch had been flipped, and there was no turning it off. She pursed her lips when he leaned in slightly, his breath warm against her ear.

"You look a little flushed. Are you feeling alright?"

She forced a tight smile, her voice a whisper. "I'm fine."

Resisting the urge to fan herself, she knew she had never spoken a bigger lie.

She was on fire.

His concern lingered in his gaze, but he nodded and turned back to the conversation. She barely heard a word. Her eyes flicked to the large windows across the dining room. She couldn't see the trawler from this angle—but she could feel it, just beyond the horizon, waiting. Beckoning. Teasing her to end this torture by putting as much distance as she could between them.

Italy.

She could go back to Italy, find a quiet harbor, and disappear until her hormones chilled out. That dream tugged at her chest, a false promise of freedom when what she really wanted was sitting right next to her, his leg brushing against hers under the table.

The Italy escape fantasy popped like a soap bubble with a loud bang when Alexandros slid a warm hand gently over her knee. His thumb was tracing slow, soothing circles.

Her skin lit up as if a match had been struck. She sucked in a shallow breath and dropped her gaze to the napkin in her lap as heat pooled low in her belly and between her legs.

He wasn't even looking at her. He was nodding along to something her grandfather said about family business, acting the picture of composed elegance.

All she could feel was the warmth of his hand through the thin material of her skirt. She didn't care about dinner, or escape, or her wildly spiraling plans to flee to another continent anymore.

She wanted this—him.

One night—to see what it could be like between them.

One chance to see if the fire between them was real—or just the residue of past trauma, fantasy, or just plain hormones.

Her fingers slid down, covering his. A breath. A choice. A sense of empowerment filled her as she guided his hand higher beneath the hem of her skirt. His fingers stilled for a heartbeat—then trembled slightly as she guided his hand between her legs, letting him feel the heat and ache he had built inside her with every restrained night in her bed.

He inhaled sharply.

She smiled sweetly at the table, eyes demurely lowered.

A heartbeat passed.

His fingers twitched when she rocked her hips ever so gently.

She felt the change in him like a jolt through the air. His hand flexed, the muscle in his thigh clenched, and the air between them thickened to something electric.

"Christ," he whispered hoarsely, barely audible.

She turned to him, her eyes laughing, teasing. Her hips shifted again, guiding his fingers in a way that made her throat catch.

He didn't look at her.

He didn't have to.

The next moment, he dropped his napkin onto the table with a clatter, pushed back his chair, and stood.

"I'd like to take Dani outside," he said, his voice rougher than usual. "To see the moonlight on the water."

There was a pause.

Eleni blinked. "But—my dear, the moon isn't even—"

"She adores the sea at night," Alexandros added smoothly, already reaching for Dani's hand.

Stuart coughed behind his wineglass. "Pretty sure moonrise isn't for another hour, but hey, who am I to argue with romance?"

Dani couldn't help it—she laughed. A breathless, giddy giggle that turned into a squeak when she was abruptly swept off her feet.

Literally.

Alexandros's arms slid under her, lifting her like she weighed nothing. Her hands flew to his shoulders for balance as he strode through the dining room, jaw tight, eyes smoldering.

Shocked murmurs and muffled laughs followed them.

He didn't stop.

Through the hall, towards the stairs, and away from the terrace. He climbed them two at a time. Her breath caught again—this time from the raw tension vibrating through his entire frame.

A muscle in his jaw ticked.

Her fingers followed, brushing his cheek. A shiver of wanton desire coursed through her.

He stopped.

Their eyes locked. Her eyes were filled with anticipation and need. His filled with a smoldering sensuality that turned her body to mush.

"You'd better understand," he said, his voice low, nearly ragged, "what is about to happen."

Her heart was thundering now, her body already trembling with the tension of yes, finally, yes.

She leaned forward, her voice barely more than a whisper. "I do."

And that was all it took.

He lowered her to her feet in the upper corridor, pushing her up against the wall. His mouth captured hers in a kiss that stole every coherent thought from her brain. There was nothing gentle about it—only heat, hunger, and the release of everything they had bottled up for far too long.

Her lips parted as she tried to catch her breath. His tongue swept inside, tangling with hers. He released her to kiss along her cheek and neck before he returned to drink deeper. His body pressed against her. His arousal strained against the thin fabric of his trousers.

His hand cupped the back of her neck, the other sliding between her thighs. She parted for him, gasping when his hand slid between the fabric of her skirt and panties and her skin. His fingers slid through the tight curls protecting her womanhood. She moaned when he caressed her swollen nub.

"Alexandros," she whimpered, pressing her face against his neck and clutching his shoulder.

"When you're near me, nothing else matters, Dani. Only you could make me lose control so much that I could take you here, in the hallway where anyone can come upon us. That tells you how much you affect me," he growled.

Her legs gave out when he stepped back. He swept her back into his arms. His face was a mask of desire. His eyes blazed with an emotion that bordered pain.

A second later, the door slammed shut behind them. She didn't recognize this room, but knew it must be his. He carried her to his bed and laid her down.

"Tell me to stop," he rasped.

"Not a chance," she whispered, tilting her head back and lifting her hands to the front of his shirt.

His lips found her neck, her collarbone, his hands sliding up her thighs, gripping, possessive and reverent all at once.

The sound of material ripping was muted by their heavy breathing. Dani frantically pulled his shirt loose from his waistband, her fingers fumbling at buttons until she could feel skin—warm and tight over muscle. He groaned when her nails scraped lightly down his stomach.

Her blouse was a lost cause. He cursed as her bra defied him. She giggled and rose far enough to lock her lips to his. She kissed him wildly, reaching back to pop the hooks free. In seconds, his hands were cupping her full breasts.

Her cry was muffled by his lips when he captured her nipples between his forefinger and thumb and pinched them.

He had been treating her like she was something precious and breakable—but his eyes told her she wasn't.

Not tonight.

Not anymore.

Tonight, she was going to be unravelled. Touched. Claimed.

And she was going to do the same to him.

Because neither of them could wait any longer.

This wasn't just fire…

It was an inferno hot enough to seal two souls into one.

ALEXANDROS SILENTLY CURSED—IN a good way. Dani was beneath him, flushed and breathless, her braid spilling across the pillows like silk. He wanted to see it unbound like her, spread out so he could bury his fingers through the silky strands.

Her eyes—wide, luminous, unguarded—searched his face, and for a moment, everything inside him stilled.

Not from hesitation.

God help him, she was beautiful. Not just her body, which was soft, fierce, and curving under his hands like it had been made for him —but the soul in her gaze. The fire. The courage. The vulnerability she never let anyone else see.

She was his. Even if she didn't know it yet.

He knew. He had known from the first moment he met her. Memories of her since their first meeting flashed through his mind. Her smile, her laughter, the twinkle of her teasing eyes. A shudder ran through him when the memory of her lying unconscious, covered in blood rose.

Never again. Never again, he thought, remembering how close he had come to losing her—losing this.

He brushed a trembling hand down her cheek. "Dani…"

Her fingers slid up, wrapping around his wrist. "Don't stop," she whispered, pressing a kiss to the inside of his wrist. "Please. I want this. I want you."

He exhaled slowly, anchoring himself in the heat of her palm. "You're so beautiful. We need to slow this down. You tell me if you want to stop. At any point."

She blinked in confusion before her cheeks flushed with color. He remembered he was her first. Her chest rose and fell as she drew in sharp little breaths.

"Maybe you should be the one telling me that because I think slow is highly overrated at the moment. You *have* no idea how much I want you—have needed you."

He leaned in until his lips brushed her ear and released a moan when her hands slipped down to the fastening of his trousers. She wasn't going to make this easy for him.

When has she? he mused before all reasonable, rational thought flew from his mind.

His lips covered hers with a sense of desperation when she tugged down his zipper and slid her hand under his boxers to wrap her hand around him.

His hips jerked forward when she began her sensual caress, sliding up and down his shaft, exploring him with a reverence that scorched him.

Nothing had ever undone him like this—like Dani. It was as if all of his nerve endings were alive. Every breath that brushed his skin, every caress sent small electrical microbursts through him. From her wild cries, Dani was experiencing the same reaction.

She gave him a brave, wobbly smile. "Love me."

Her two words hit him like a strike to the chest—raw, undeniable.

He captured her lips—not with hunger, not with desperation, but with devotion. His lips moved slowly, savoring hers, coaxing her open, letting her feel every ounce of the emotion he hadn't dared speak aloud.

She arched into him, her hands sliding up his back. Her fingertips explored the muscles there as if she was memorizing every inch. Her sigh was soft, a melody of surrender and wonder, and it made his pulse roar.

He kissed her throat, the hollow beneath her ear, and the sweet curve of her jaw. His hand slid across her bare skin, brushing a delicate path to her stomach. He rose far enough to strip the rest of his clothes off. Dani sat up, reaching for him. He grabbed her hand and brought it to his lips with a wry smile and a shake of his head.

"Right now, it has to be all about your pleasure," he said.

Confusion darkened her eyes. "Why?"

"Because I won't last long if you keep touching me. Give me this. I… need to love you. You can have your wicked way with me afterwards, I promise."

She wriggled slightly, shrugging off her torn blouse and bra before she reached up and pulled the band from the end of her braid. She ran her fingers through her hair, loosening it before she laid back and lifted her hips in invitation.

He reached down, pulling her skirt and panties off. Standing back, he caught his first, full sight of her naked on his bed, her dark auburn hair spread across his pillows like he had dreamed about, her arms above her head, and her eyes beckoning him like a siren.

"Se thélo me káthe kommáti tis psychís mou," he whispered, reverence in his voice. "I want you with every piece of my soul."

Her breath hitched. "Well, you'd better hurry, because I'm not sure how long I can keep my hands off you."

He gave a low, rough laugh. "I'm going to take my time," he teased, crawling over her to press a kiss to her shoulder. "Because you deserve everything, Dani. And I'm going to give it to you. Until you scream my name." He kissed her behind her ear, lowering his body so she could feel how aroused he was. "Over and over."

She blushed. God, it was adorable.

Her fingers tightened around his forearm. Her chest rose and fell in quick, shallow gasps, her skin flushed from her collarbones to her cheeks as he lowered his mouth and pressed a kiss over her heart before teasing each nipple until they were taut pebbles.

She moaned—soft, shocked.

It almost undid him.

With aching restraint, he kissed his way down her ribs, pausing at the scar on her side where Zayan had stabbed her. He ran his lips along it.

A shudder ran through her, and she arched into him, threading her fingers through his hair.

"Not yet. Don't touch me... yet, *kardiá mou*," he instructed hoarsely.

"But... I want you!"

"Soon, *agápi mou*. You must come first," he promised.

He slid down her hips, kissing each newly revealed inch as she lay bare before him. Her thighs trembled, her eyes dark with desire and frustration at the building tension.

He was painfully conscious of how close he was to losing control—but he had to make this perfect. This wasn't just about lust. This was about everything he hadn't said yet.

Sliding his hands under her thighs, he lifted her hips. Before she could question what he was doing, he revealed her sweet nub and feasted. Her breathless cries filled his soul with pleasure. She twisted and turned, fighting the intense sensations ricocheting through her body while marveling at it.

"Alexandros!" she wailed, her body bucking as he tortured her engorged clitoris.

Her breathing became more erratic as he brushed his tongue over her and sucked. His grip on her thighs tightened when she began to tremble uncontrollably, and he knew she was about to come. Her body bowed, her heels pressed into his lower back, and her thighs clamped around his head as she came in one long, delicious orgasm.

Her fingers clutched the bedsheets until her knuckles were white. A soft whimper escaped her lips as he pulled away. She would have to wait to explore his body. He knew he wouldn't last if she touched him.

Rising over her, he settled between her legs, skin to skin, their bodies lined up like puzzle pieces that had waited too long to be joined, he held himself still—just barely resting against her heat.

"Dani." His voice was rough. "It might hurt for a moment, but I swear—I'll go slow. Just breathe with me. Trust me, *kardiá mou*."

She nodded, eyes luminous.

"I trust you," she whispered. "I want this with you, Alexandros."

He bit back a groan. "*S'agapó*, Dani. I love you, *kardiá mou*."

He kissed her again—slowly and deeply—as he pressed forward.

He moved carefully, filling her, giving her time, giving himself time, though every cell in his body screamed for more. He forced himself to breathe when he felt the thin barrier. His body trembled when Dani shifted her hips, pressing him deeper.

"Ah, Dani. Ah, *moro mou*."

He groaned as her body adjusted around him. Fully. Possessed. He drew a ragged breath. Home.

She was tight, slick, warm, and clenching around him like she'd been made for no one else. He held still, shaking with the effort, every muscle taut with restraint.

She breathed against his throat.

One breath.

Then another.

He whispered to her softly—Greek endearments, sweet nonsense, anything to soothe her.

When she finally relaxed, he began to move.

Slowly at first. Testing. Easing her into the rhythm.

She gasped. Then moaned.

Her hips shifted to meet his.

He nearly lost it right then and there.

"Dani," he choked. "You feel like heaven."

She clung to him. Her eyes glazed with pleasure. "Don't stop. Please, whatever you do, don't stop."

He didn't—couldn't even if he wanted to. He was beyond all rational thought. His focus was centered on the woman in his arms, the sounds of her breathless moans, the pleasure enveloping them.

Their rhythm built—gentle, then urgent. Moans turned into cries. Touches turned into grasps. Love whispered itself between kisses, between thrusts. Not spoken aloud, but felt in every touch, every sigh, every shuddering breath.

When she climaxed again, it was fierce, breathtaking—beautiful. The heat exploded through Alexandros like a star going nova. He knew it would be powerful, knew it would shake him—but he wasn't prepared for the way it shattered him completely.

Minutes afterwards, his body still shuddered with the aftermath of his release. His cock still hard, throbbing against Dani's silken channel. He held her tightly, stroking her hair, their bodies tangled in a sheen of sweat and moonlight.

She nestled against him, sated and safe.

"I love you, Danika. I love you with every fiber of my being," he whispered, burying his face in her hair.

She didn't answer.

But her hand curled against his chest, right over his heart.

And that was enough—for now.

CHAPTER 14

The soft rise and fall of Alexandros's chest as he breathed was the only sound in the room. His face—so calm, so heartbreakingly at peace—felt like a punch to her ribs.

Dani stood at the edge of the bed, barely breathing, her fingers clenched the soft canvas knapsack she had slung over her shoulder. Her body still hummed from the night before—her thighs ached, her lips tingled... and her chest ached like it might crack open.

Tears blurred her vision as she stared at the man she loved.

Loved.

She did. She loved him.

And that was why she had to go.

She pressed her knuckles to her mouth, choking back the sob rising in her throat. His scent still clung to her skin—dark, woodsy, intimate. His touch already a ghost she'd never be able to outrun.

Last night had been more than she ever imagined. More than just sex. It had been a deeper connection, one that had touched her all the way to her soul. She had surrendered to feelings she knew but didn't understand—until now.

It terrified her.

Once, she had dreamed of a love like this. The kind that wrapped around her bones and made her believe in forever. The kind her grandfather had felt for her grandmother. The kind her parents had shared.

It was the nightmare of that love that had woken her, feeling queasy and panicked.

Look how that ended.

Her throat tightened.

Pain speared her again—but this time, she let it in.

She could still hear their laughter—hers and her parents'—as they planned their vacation. Then came the screams, tearing through her memory like the moment it all fell apart.

She closed her eyes. She could almost feel the flames. Smell the smoke. Hear her mother's anguished, pain-filled screams. Feel the weight of her father's silence.

For years, there had only been charred pieces of memory, relived in fragmented nightmares. But the soft, broken sound of her mother's weeping, her tortured pleas, had haunted her dreams.

Dani finally understood the answer that had always been there—in the shadows. She understood why her mother's heart—her very desire to live—simply gave out. It stemmed from the pain of losing the man she loved more than life itself.

Her grandfather had tried. He'd held her, comforted her, offered reasons that never soothed the ache. The therapist had done the same. But nothing could stop the weight of her grief—or her fear.

Her mom might have made it if her dad had lived.

That was love, Dani thought bitterly. *A beautiful dream that could turn into a nightmare in an instant, leaving you vulnerable—defenseless.*

She used to think love could heal. That was why she'd trusted Zayan—because he offered the illusion of it. He had made her forget for a short while.

But true love—genuine love—doesn't make you forget. It makes you realize how much you have to lose, she thought with a twist of agony.

The thought of losing Alexandros—whether it was in five years or fifty—was unbearable. The idea of waking up one morning and not having him beside her, of hearing his laugh vanish, of watching the light in his eyes dim forever?

No. She couldn't survive it.

She wouldn't survive it.

She would rather walk away now. While she still could.

With trembling fingers, she reached out to brush his hair back from his forehead, but paused before she touched him, afraid of waking him up. Her vision swam. His skin would be warm under her touch. The faintest smile still ghosted his lips, as if he was dreaming of her.

"I'm sorry," she whispered. "I love you too much."

She stepped back on silent feet, careful not to disturb him. Her knees threatened to buckle beneath her, but she forced herself to stay upright. Her clothes from the night before were crumpled in a heap on the floor, but she ignored them. They were ruined—like her. Unfixable. Torn between what was and what would never be again.

She turned away, crossing the room. She picked up her boots by the door before adjusting the knapsack she'd packed before dinner last night.

The fact that she'd packed it was proof she was making the right decision. She'd known, deep down, she wouldn't be able to stay. Not after spending the night with Alexandros. Not after feeling what actual love was. Not when the risk of losing it was so unbearably high.

The hallway was silent.

Cool air brushed her face as she stepped barefoot onto the marble floors. Each step sent her boots tapping against her knee like a warning bell—each knock a whisper: *Don't do this.*

She padded quietly past the guest bedrooms, hearing her grandfather's familiar snores as she passed a room two doors down. She continued down the staircase and into the foyer lit only by the faint orange glow of a single table lamp.

The villa was asleep. She would still have to be careful. She knew the family had added additional security—especially after what had happened to her.

Outside, the sky was still cloaked in deep navy, stars twinkling overhead. The smell of saltwater filled her lungs as she crept across the stone terrace, staying in the shadows and out of range of the security cameras. She followed the gravel path to the boathouse.

She glanced back only once.

The villa stood proudly against the hills, bathed in shadow and moonlight. Somewhere inside, Alexandros was still sleeping. Safe. Beautiful. Unaware.

Her heart cracked.

"I'm so sorry," she whispered again, then turned away.

Inside the boathouse, the air was cool and damp. The little aluminum dinghy was tied loosely to the dock. She untied the rope with numb fingers, shoving the small boat into the dark water with a quiet desperation that felt almost like a prayer. It bobbed in the surf like it too was unsure of her decision.

She slipped into it quietly and grabbed the oars.

Each stroke was slow and steady, the dip and pull of the paddles slicing through the water with soft splashes that seemed far too loud in the silence.

It took longer than she expected to reach *The Gentle Breeze*, anchored just offshore. The sea rocked the dinghy as she tied it off and climbed the ladder to the deck, her limbs trembling with each step. The moment her boots hit the wood, her knees buckled.

This was it.

No turning back.

She pushed up, holding onto the side before she walked on numb legs to the wheelhouse, blinking furiously to clear her tears. With practiced movements, she pulled the bow and stern anchors. The trawler shifted, weightless again.

Her gaze turned toward the villa. She could still see it there, nestled on the slope, lights twinkling like fireflies in the dark. The bedroom windows were dark.

Goodbye.

She bit her lip, trying to keep the sobs from carrying over the water. There would be time for tears later. She would let them wash the pain away—she hoped.

Turning away, she powered on the engines. They purred to life—betraying her with their obedience, when all she wanted was a reason to stay.

By the time the horizon began to soften with the first kiss of dawn, *The Gentle Breeze* cruised silently through the inter-coastal waterway. Dani gripped the wheel with trembling hands, steering away from the only man she knew she would ever love.

Her chest ached, every heartbeat cracking something deeper.

She was doing the right thing.

Aren't I?

Better to leave before love turned to ashes.

Better to run than risk breaking the way her mother had.

Better to drift into the unknown alone than be wrecked on the shores of grief again.

But even as she told herself that… the tears wouldn't stop falling.

And neither would the whisper in her soul begging her to turn around.

ALEXANDROS PROWLED the floor of his office. His assistant was talking about corporate acquisitions—deals, expansions, numbers. None of it mattered. Not since the morning he woke up and found Dani gone.

He didn't care about acquisitions. He cared only about one thing—the woman who vanished from his bed three weeks ago. The one who haunted his every waking thought.

He turned when the door to his office suddenly opened. Theo entered first, his expression grim but laced with a glint of triumph. Demetrius followed, silent, a plain manila folder in his hand. He held it out without a word.

Alexandros's jaw tightened, and he dismissed Julius with a sharp nod.

She had disappeared without a note. Without a goodbye. Without a trace.

Just her scent on his skin... and a hollow where his heart used to be.

His world hadn't just tilted. It had shattered—and he was still walking through the wreckage. He needed to know why.

He snatched the folder from Demetrius's outstretched hand and turned toward the tall windows overlooking the Athens skyline. The city shimmered beneath a late afternoon haze, distant and indifferent.

"She's been hiding under our noses," Demetrius said, a hint of amazement in his voice. "The entire time."

Alexandros didn't look at him. He flipped open the folder.

Photos. Satellite timestamps. Port authority logs. Names he didn't recognize. And then—her name. Only tweaked slightly.

Rae Bouras.

His lips pulled into a hard line.

The first report hit like a punch. Dani had taken *The Gentle Breeze* to a marina in Italy—Porto di Livorno—just two days after disappearing. She'd left the trawler docked there under the pretense of engine issues, paid in cash, and vanished.

Two days later, she'd signed onto a private yacht crew. The Valdez. Registered in the Caymans. It had set sail for the Athenian Riviera... and remained anchored there for the last two weeks.

He turned the next page.

His heart stopped.

A mechanic's log entry. The handwriting was hers, even if the name read Rae Bouras. A new marina. A new life.

A lie.

She was working on marine engines again—beneath his nose— while he'd been combing the globe. While he hadn't slept. While his mother had wept, and Stuart had made excuses, and Theo had driven half of Europe searching.

His hand clenched the folder so tightly the plastic sleeve crinkled.

"Is she under surveillance?" His voice was low. Controlled.

"Yes," Demetrius replied. "We've had eyes on her since last night. Stuart's got his own guy—or I should say gal—on her, too. I suspect he knew where she was all the time."

At the mention of Stuart's name, Alexandros turned. Fury burned in his eyes.

Of course, the old man knew. He had the resources and knew Dani better than anyone.

The question was why had he let her run?

Why hadn't Stuart told him? Not just that Dani was safe—but where she was. Why had he let him believe he didn't know?

"Pull the car around," Alexandros said tightly.

Demetrius bowed slightly and left without another word.

Theo lingered, arms crossed. "Want me to come with you?"

Alexandros shook his head, his jaw rigid. "No."

Theo studied him for a moment, then gave a dry laugh. "This is why I'm never falling in love. Women are too much trouble. You aren't going to throttle her, are you?"

A breath passed through Alexandros's nose—half agreement, half agony.

"She's not just trouble," he said hoarsely. "She's everything. And no, I won't throttle her—but I might just tie her to the bed."

Theo chuckled and gave Alexandros's shoulder a solid slap. "I'll keep Nikos on her until you do."

Alexandros grunted a response, watching his brother turn and walk out.

Alone in the office, Alexandros stood still, the folder dangling from his fingers.

Three weeks.

Three weeks of torment. Of waking up with his arms empty. Of reaching across the sheets to cold linens. Of smelling her on his skin and clothes like she was an apparition who was there but he couldn't see.

Three weeks of cursing himself for not waking when she'd slipped away.

Three weeks of fury and fear, braided so tightly they hollowed out his ribs like ghosts he couldn't outrun.

He stared out at the skyline, his reflection faint in the glass.

She had run from him.

But she hadn't vanished.

And now… now he had found her.

No more distance. No more shadows.

No more excuses.

He lifted his phone, pressed in a number, and waited as he strode out of his office to the elevator. The call was answered on the first ring. He breathed down the anger coursing through him. He needed to remain calm.

"Why didn't you tell me she was safe? Why didn't you tell me where she was?" he demanded, skipping the greeting entirely.

Stuart's loud sigh echoed in his ear. "If I told you she was safe, you'd know I knew where she was. She wasn't ready to be found. And if I recall, you weren't exactly calm either after she disappeared."

"That doesn't answer my question. Why, Stuart? Why did she run? Why didn't you tell me?"

"I can't answer why she ran. Only Dani can answer that. What I think and what I know are two different things. You need to get Dani to open up to you—if she will. The only thing I do know is that she is scared."

Alexandros stiffened and paused as the lift slowed and opened into the underground car park.

"She is scared—of me?" he asked.

His gut twisted at the thought of Dani being afraid of him. He would never hurt her. She… she was his world. It was his job—his right—to protect her from harm.

"Not of you—but I think for you. Ask her. I knew you would find her when the time was right," Stuart said, before he ended the call.

Alexandros lowered his phone, his mind tormented by what Stuart had left unsaid.

"Scared for me?" he echoed, the words slicing through him. "Why would she be scared for me?"

He slid into the back seat of the black BMW SUV. Demetrius was behind the wheel. The tinted windows shielded him from the sun. But nothing could block the fire building inside him now.

No more running, Dani. Not this time. Never again.

CHAPTER 15

The scent of oil and sun-warmed wood clung to the air, mingling with the metallic tang of grease and sea salt. Overhead, a gull screeched, its cry slicing through the low hum of chatter from men swapping stories in the shade. Someone had a radio on, playing a popular Greek pop song, the beat bounced off the corrugated metal walls of the workshop. But Dani didn't hear it.

Her world was muffled. Muted. Her mind was a million miles away—or at least it felt like it. In truth, it was more like just a few miles as the crow flies. Depending on where Alexandros was at the moment—his office, his apartment, or the villa.

She leaned forward, trying to focus on what she was supposed to be working on. She was currently elbow-deep in the guts of a temperamental diesel engine hoisted on chains, the familiar grind of metal against metal echoing her mood. Her arms ached, her hands were raw beneath her gloves, and sweat clung to her spine.

She didn't mind.

The work was physical, consuming—one of the few things that kept her from unraveling completely.

But it didn't stop the ache. Nothing stopped the ache.

The worst part wasn't the silence—it was the relentless throb of her breaking heart. Night after night, the ache came like clockwork, hollowing her out until she forgot what peace felt like.

She'd lost weight. She could feel it in her bones. No amount of makeup could hide the shadows beneath her eyes. The boys in the yard had stopped teasing her after the first week. Now they just left coffee on the workbench and kept their distance.

She didn't blame them.

She wasn't good company.

Today was no better. Her stomach churn and her thoughts were a mess of wrenching memories and half-formed regrets. Her hands paused on the socket wrench. She flexed her fingers to stop the trembling.

"Dani, *mou!*"

She blinked and turned. Maria's voice broke through her fog, bright and sweet like a bell.

She smiled as the other woman wove her way through the rows of boats and benches, her dark hair swept into a messy knot, a paper bag held high like a peace offering.

Dani felt the corner of her mouth twitch. Despite everything, Maria's energy was infectious.

"I brought your favorite," Maria announced proudly, waving the bag. "Prosciutto, arugula, fig jam on that rustic olive bread you love. Still warm."

Dani pulled off her gloves, wiped her hands on a rag, and crossed to meet her friend.

They kissed on each cheek, the familiar greeting grounding her more than she cared to admit.

"I thought you were done with feeding me," Dani teased weakly, trying to summon a genuine smile.

"I'm half-Greek. Feeding the people we love is practically our love language."

Dani's stomach twisted, not with hunger but with something closer to dread.

She took the bag with a grateful nod but didn't open it. Her fingers went still.

Maria kept chatting—something about a café she'd discovered, a new job lead—but her words blurred at the edges as Dani stared at the paper sack.

That sandwich.

It wasn't just a favorite—it was comfort food. Her comfort food. One only her grandfather ever made—making it for the first time after he had purchased the trawler.

Her fingers tightened.

Maria's voice faltered. "Dani? Is everything okay?"

Dani looked up slowly, her voice quieter than her expression. "How long have you been working undercover for my grandfather?"

Maria blinked. "What? I don't—"

Her friend's eyes darted to the bag, realization dawning in slow motion.

She sighed. "Damn. I was hoping you wouldn't notice."

"So, it's true."

Maria shrugged one shoulder, the movement half apology, half resignation. "Stuart asked me to keep an eye on you. Just... make sure you were okay. I didn't lie to you, Dani. I just didn't tell you everything."

Dani nodded, her throat tightening. "And Carlos?"

Maria hesitated. Then, quietly, "He's one of Stuart's men too. Been working security on and off for him for years."

A bitter laugh slipped from Dani's lips, jagged and empty. She turned away, staring out at the boats bobbing in the marina. Sunlight danced across the rippling water—mockingly cheerful.

"Does he know where I am?" she asked, her voice slightly uneven. "Alexandros?"

Maria didn't answer. She didn't have to.

Dani looked down at the paper bag again, the sandwich now a symbol of everything she couldn't avoid. Her hands trembled as she held it out to Maria.

"Here. You eat it."

"Dani…"

"I'm not angry," she murmured. "Just… tired. Tired of pretending everything's fine. Tired of holding myself together with duct tape and lies…"

Maria's eyes searched hers, worry creasing her brow. "Where are you going?"

Dani collected her tools, picked up her tool bag, and slung it over her shoulder with practiced ease. Her body was on autopilot, but her heart had already made the choice.

"If you don't mind, I'd like you to hang out here for a while. If-if Alexandros shows up, tell him I'll meet him where we started."

Maria's brows drew together. "Where you started?"

Dani nodded. "Trust me—he'll know."

Without waiting for a reply, she turned and walked down the workshop aisle, boots echoing against the concrete like the slow beat of a war drum.

The sun hit her face as she stepped outside. Salt air filled her lungs, clearing her head.

She spotted Yiorgos, the old fisherman who always let her borrow his boat when he didn't need it.

"Need a lift, *koukla*?" he asked, eyeing her bag.

She smiled faintly. "Yeah. If you don't mind."

He nodded toward his boat. "Hop in. It is a beautiful day to be on the water. Add in a beautiful woman, and my life is complete!"

Dani laughed and climbed into the boat, her heart pounding louder than the engine as it rumbled to life.

She dropped her tool bag onto the deck and sat down on the bench seat in front of the center console as Yiorgos chatted and idled the boat into the channel. In the distance, Dani could see where the yacht—his yacht—was anchored. Waiting.

She didn't know what she would say when she saw him again. She didn't know what he would do.

But she knew one thing.

She was done hiding.

Even if it broke her.

She was going to face the man she loved and all her demons.

And the best place to do it was where they began.

~

THE SALTY WIND hit Alexandros the moment he stepped out of the SUV, his eyes narrowing against the glare bouncing off the Aegean. The marina bustled with the usual hum of fishermen and tourists, but Alexandros moved through it like a force of nature—focused, sharp, barely leashed.

Nikos, Theo's steely-eyed man, was already waiting at the edge of the dock. Luca, one of Demetrius's guys, stood just behind him, arms folded, face unreadable. Both straightened the moment they saw him.

"She's gone," Nikos said without preamble. "Left about twenty minutes ago in a skiff with an old man named Yiorgos. Fisherman. Local." He nodded toward the open sea. "Heading that way."

A curse hissed through Alexandros's teeth as he glared at the sunlit water stretching endlessly before him. "Damn it."

He turned back toward the SUV, his jaw tight with frustration. Then he saw her.

A lone woman stood outside the open bay Dani had been working in, her black hair pulled back, a paper bag dangling from her hand. Recognition struck immediately. Maria Sanchez. The security agent from Stuart's dossier. The one assigned to Dani without Alexandros's knowledge.

He stormed toward her, gravel crunching under his expensive leather shoes.

"What did she say?" he demanded.

Maria didn't flinch. Her expression was calm, but her eyes were searching his, as if weighing her loyalty to protect Dani or Dani's wishes to convey her message.

"She told me to tell you," Maria said gently, "that she'll meet you where it all began."

Alexandros stilled.

Then, slowly, his gaze turned back toward the water. A realization flickered in his stormy eyes.

A smile—not soft, not amused, but sharp and knowing—curved his lips.

He pivoted sharply. "Demetrius." His tone cracked like a whip.

The other man appeared instantly at his side.

"Ten thousand euros to anyone who can get me to my yacht— now," Alexandros said, his voice like steel.

Demetrius blinked. "Yes, sir."

Word traveled fast.

Within seconds, a dozen offers were shouted across the pier. Alexandros scanned the hopeful faces and picked the sturdiest-looking vessel among them— a weathered old taxi boat with cracked paint and a captain who didn't blink at a bribe.

He climbed aboard with Demetrius close behind, gripping the rails as the boat shuddered to life and surged away from the marina.

The ride was rougher than he liked. The sea was choppy, the wind rising with the late afternoon sun, but none of it mattered.

All he saw was the gleaming silhouette of the *Kallistratos Challenge* —his yacht, his fortress, his sanctuary—anchored in the distance.

A member of his security greeted them at the stern. Alexandros vaulted onto the platform with practiced ease. The moment his feet hit the teakwood deck, one of his crew approached, tipping his cap nervously.

"Ms. Bouras arrived ten, fifteen minutes ago. She asked for the stateroom… downstairs. She said you would be expecting her," the man said.

Alexandros didn't answer.

His feet were already moving.

He took the stairs two at a time, his suit jacket flaring behind him. A steward rounding the corner yelped and flattened himself against the wall. Alexandros didn't stop.

His pulse thundered as he neared the stateroom.

That stateroom.

Memories flashed through his mind as he remembered the first time he laid eyes on her. She was his fiery mermaid, dressed in an ill-fitting sequined red evening gown. She had the mouth of a sailor and the lightning fist of a prizefighter, but it was her mischievous eyes that beckoned to him—snared his heart.

He reached for the handle and pushed the door open with one steady breath.

The elegant room looked vacant at first. The accent lights cast a soft golden light across the pristinely made bed. The hum of the environmental system, keeping the ambient temperature perfect for visitors.

His gaze swept the room. Dani's beloved tool bag lay on the floor like a breadcrumb left for him.

His pulse sped up when he followed the other crumbs she had left. Clothes trailed across the carpet—jeans, a wrinkled t-shirt, a single sock.

He was almost to the in-suite bathroom when the door opened. Steam curled like mist around the vision emerging. Her slender form silhouetted by the bathroom light. His heart clenched when she paused in the doorway.

Dani.

She clutched a dark blue towel to her chest. Strands of her damp, auburn hair clung to her cheeks, vibrant and sensual, making him think she really was a mermaid come to life. Her eyes widened the moment she saw him. As her lips parted, he heard the soft catch in her breath, a delicate sound that spoke volumes of her emotions.

He didn't move. Couldn't.

The world stopped. He had dreamed of this moment for the past three weeks only to wake to the nightmare that she was gone. The damp towel slipped from her grasp, falling silently to the floor. His gaze devoured every inch of her, lingering on the curve of her lips before traveling down her body.

In the space of a heartbeat, she closed the distance. Her hands flew to his face, her fingers cupping his cheeks as her lips crashed against his.

She kissed him like a woman surfacing after being lost at sea—

gasping, desperate, alive. Like he was the last breath she needed to live.

Alexandros groaned, catching her waist as he stumbled back. Her mouth moved against his with wild, desperate hunger, all teeth and gasps and tears.

Her hands tore at his suit jacket, yanking it off his shoulders. She pulled his linen shirt from his trousers and pushed it up, her hands sliding under it to caress his heated flesh. He pulled at his shirt with one hand, impatiently ripping the buttons off so he could shrug out of it. Nothing else existed—only the feel of her skin against his.

She tasted like warm honey and tears and every dream he'd ever denied himself.

He toed off his shoes, kicking them to the side. Dani had unfastened his belt, trousers, and zipper. Her hands pushed down on his boxers and trousers until they slid to his ankles.

He fell back onto the bed with a curse, his breath hissing out of him as she climbed up on top of him and straddled his waist. Her eyes were glazed with emotion.

He tried to speak. To ask her why. Where she had been. If she was okay.

If she was staying.

His questions died unspoken as she silenced him, her lips finding his in a kiss that stole his breath away. This kiss was rougher, deeper, a desperate collision of lips and breath, tasting of urgency and longing —pain and hope. Her hands, calloused yet soft, braced against the firm muscles of his chest even as her thighs tightened around his hips.

She lifted her body, reaching down between them to wrap her hand around his throbbing shaft. She guided him with trembling fingers, and with a long, aching moan... she took him in.

Fully. Completely. Without hesitation.

Impaling herself while arching her back and throwing her head back, thrusting her breasts forward with a long moan of need and pleasure.

Alexandros gasped, his hands clutching her hips as her body trembled above his. Her head dropped forward, her forehead resting against his as her breath came in soft, broken pants. She began to move, rising and falling on him in deep, desperate strokes, as if she was afraid he would disappear.

He kept one hand on her hip and reached up to thread his hand through her hair with the other. He kissed, slowing her movements because he knew he wouldn't last. He slowed their frenzied pace, drawing it out, calming her wild emotions. He wanted to show her with every touch that she was safe now. That she was his.

"I *need* you," Dani whispered, the words breaking in half. "I've missed you so much."

"You have me, Dani. I won't let you go. Never again, *agápi mou*. You are my love." He kissed her. "*Psíchi mou*. My soul." His lips captured hers again. "*Kardiá mou*. My heart, Danika. Always and forever."

"I can't lose you. Not like-like—"

Tears slipped down her cheeks, and she kissed him again as if she were terrified of losing him. He kicked off his trousers that were still wrapped around his ankles, knowing that Dani didn't need slow and gentle right now.

She moved against him with a rhythm born of longing and agony, her nails digging into his shoulders, her voice a soft, breathy sob against his skin.

Each movement shattered him. Rebuilt him.

Every part of him ached with the need to protect her, to never let her go again.

He whispered her name. Over and over.

Like a vow.

Like a prayer.

And when she cried out his name, her body shuddering in release, he held her tightly before rolling them over until she was under him. Only then did he release his tight grip on his control and give in to his own fear and desperate need. He held her tight, his breaths coming in deep gasps as he took her until he swore he could feel the tip of his cock brush her womb. Sweat beaded on his brow and he gritted his teeth, groaning loudly through them as he found his peace. Hot jets of his seed pulsed deep into Dani, marking her, sealing their fates. She was his—now and forever.

He released a hoarse, fierce cry. His body trembled with the force of his release.

"You're mine," he breathed, fierce and unyielding. "No more running. Not from me. Never again."

CHAPTER 16

*T*wilight wrapped the room in a hush, the kind that made the world feel far away. Faint light filtered from the bathroom, casting shadows that danced across the stateroom. The faint scent of soap and Alexandros lingered in the air where they had showered earlier, only to return to bed again before they could get dressed.

Dani lay curled against his side, her cheek pressed to the steady rise and fall of his chest. One of his hands traced slow, lazy circles along her spine, the motion soothing and unhurried, as if he had all the time in the world to touch her.

She wanted to stay in this moment forever.

But she knew he deserved answers.

Her chest tightened.

Her chest tightened as a phantom ache curled low in her stomach, rising from something old and buried. Her muscles tensed before she could stop it. The memories came too fast. Too sharp.

Alexandros felt it immediately.

He didn't speak at first, didn't ask what was wrong. He wrapped his arms around her, tucking her beneath his chin, his hand spread protectively over her hip.

His breath was warm against her hair when he finally whispered, "Why did you run, Dani?"

"You have no idea what that did to me," he murmured. "Why would you leave me? I was terrified something would happen—and I wouldn't be there to stop it."

Her lips trembled.

She didn't answer right away—her throat too tight to speak.

His arms stayed around her, firm and patient, like he could hold back the ghosts just by not letting go.

"I do know," she whispered at last. "I know exactly how that fear feels. All too well."

He said nothing—waiting for her to continue.

She closed her eyes, breathing him in, grounding herself in his warmth before the words came—soft, faltering at first, then gathering strength like a river breaking through a dam.

"My parents were happy," she began. "The kind of happy that made other people smile just watching them. They were best friends. Soulmates. They did everything together—not because they had to... but because they couldn't imagine not being near each other. It was like watching two halves of a whole."

She felt him nod against her hair, his hand still stroking her back.

"When they looked at each other, it was like... like they were seeing the most beautiful thing in the world. Every single time. When they were apart, even for a few hours, the reunion was always... radiant. Their smiles—God, it was like the sun came out just for them."

Alexandros's voice was rough. "My parents are like that too. Theo and I used to make fun of them. We told them they were setting an impossible standard... how could anyone ever live up to a love like that?"

Dani smiled faintly, but it faded just as fast.

"Everything changed when I was fifteen," she said quietly. "We were flying to a remote lake house in Alaska for a summer break. My dad was a pilot. He flew us to different places all the time. It wasn't supposed to be a big deal. Just us, two weeks off the grid, with mountains, fishing, and hot cocoa made on a dumb wood-burning stove that never worked right."

Her fingers curled against Alexandros's ribs.

"We'd only been in the air thirty minutes when something went wrong. An engine light. A sputter. I remember my dad's voice going tight. Calm, but clipped. He said we needed to return to the airfield. He promised that everything was going to be fine."

Her voice hitched. "But it wasn't. It never would be again."

Alexandros's arms tightened around her. Still silent. Still listening.

"The plane clipped the top of the trees before it crashed into the mountain. I don't even remember the impact—just the sound. Metal screaming. My body hit something hard. Then pain."

She paused. Took a breath that felt stale and tight in her lungs.

"My arm was broken, and I had bruised ribs and several deep cuts. I was lucky. My dad…" Her voice cracked. "He died on impact."

A tear slipped down her cheek, soaking into Alexandros's skin. He continued caressing her, soothing her. He was her light in the darkness.

"My mom was still alive," Dani whispered. "A tree branch pierced the windshield. It impaled her side. She was conscious. In shock. Bleeding out. But still fighting. She was calling to him. Reaching for him like… like she could pull him back just by touching him."

Her breath hitched again.

"I tried to help her. Tried to calm her down. But she just kept… breaking. Her breathing got worse. She said life without him would be too empty. That her heart wasn't strong enough to stay."

She buried her face in his chest, her tears burning hot and fast.

"She slipped into unconsciousness shortly before the rescue team arrived. She never woke up."

Alexandros's hand moved up to cradle the back of her head, his thumb stroking her temple as she sobbed.

"I was only fifteen," she choked. "I needed them both, but if I couldn't have both, at least one. I watched my mother give up because her heart was too broken to go on."

Her words dropped into the silence like stones in a still pond.

"I'm terrified, Alexandros," she confessed. "Of loving someone that much. Of losing them. Because I know what it looks like... I know what it feels like when love breaks you. It doesn't just hurt—it undoes you. And I—I don't think I could survive that again."

He kissed her hair. Once. Twice.

She clung to him.

"I didn't run because I didn't love you," she whispered. "I ran because I do. I love you so very much."

Her words were muffled against his chest, but they vibrated through him all the same.

For a long moment, neither of them moved. He just held her, like he could absorb her grief, her fear—all the years she'd spent burying her pain.

When he spoke, his voice came—low, fierce, and full of devotion.

"I'm not your past, Dani," he murmured. "You're not alone anymore. I will love you the way you deserve to be loved. Steady. Certain. Every day. For as long as I can. There are no guarantees in life, but if it's within my power, I'll stay by your side for all of it. And... if I can't, or you—." He drew a deep breath before he continued. "I want you to know that every single second I have with you would be worth the pain because the love I feel for you is too great to deny."

He shifted, tilting her face up to his, brushing the tears from her cheeks with his thumbs.

"So fall," he whispered. "Fall in love with me. Take the chance... I'll catch you. Every damn time."

She looked into his eyes—and saw no fear, no hesitation.

Just love.

And this time, she didn't run.

She let herself fall—and Alexandros's love caught her.

THE GENTLE CHUG-CHUG-CHUG of the engine blended with the rhythmic slap of waves against the hull of *The Gentle Breeze*. Alexandros leaned back against the bench seat, a glass of wine in hand and the sun warm against his chest. Dani sat next to him, guiding the trawler through the channel. She reached across him for another piece of the peeled clementines he had placed in a bowl for them to snack on.

Her fingers were sticky and orange-scented, and he wanted to lick the juice off. He knew if he did that they would have to anchor out of the channel because it would never stop with him licking just her fingers.

He couldn't take his eyes off her.

She was laughing—laughing—with that low, throaty sound that made his stomach tighten. She'd just finished telling a ridiculous story about slipping into the water at the marina while trying to impress a group of retired fishermen with her knot-tying skills.

"They still tease me about it," she said, popping a piece of fruit into her mouth. "I swear Kostas told the story four times before lunch."

"They adore you," Alexandros said, smiling. "Even the one with three teeth."

"Ah, Spiro," she chuckled. "He keeps offering to find me a 'nice Greek husband' who can build me a fishing boat from scratch."

Alexandros arched a brow. "Should I be worried?"

She licked her lips and studied him with a sultry expression. "Jealous, Mr. Kallistratos?"

He leaned forward, plucked a piece of clementine from her fingers, and said, "Terribly. But I hear you're already quite taken with a Greek man who owns a ludicrously large yacht and scowls like a storm cloud when he catches you driving too fast on that scooter from hell you own."

She laughed again and shoved his shoulder. "I was going fourteen kilometers an hour. That's barely faster than a jog."

"I have seen death glare at me with less intensity than your Vespa."

She rolled her eyes, but her grin softened as she tilted her face to the fading shafts of sunlight. The wind tugged at her hair, wild and fiery in the light. Sun-kissed and barefoot, she looked more like a sea nymph than a billionaire's heir.

No one would guess who she was.

Alexandros didn't care. She was his Danika. His mermaid. His mechanic. His lover. And he hoped that soon he could add his wife to the list.

He loved this version of her. He would never tire of watching her barter with dockhands, flirt information out of grumpy mechanics, and chat with fishermen about carburetors and fishing lines as if she'd been born to the sea.

He still remembered the way she'd waved goodbye to the marina crew two weeks earlier, oil-stained gloves hanging from her belt like a badge of honor.

They'd spent nearly a week on his yacht, giving Dani time to finish the engine repair she'd promised at the marina. He'd pretended to protest, but truthfully, it had been some of his favorite days—sitting nearby, sipping espresso, reading reports half-heartedly while sneaking glances at her bent over an engine block, her hair twisted into a messy knot and her tank top clinging to her back in the heat.

He hadn't taken this much time off work in... ever.

He didn't miss it.

Not the boardrooms.

Not the meetings.

Not the women.

He looked at Dani now and felt the same fierce surge of something he didn't have a name for until she'd walked into his life.

Love.

He was in love. And not in the way he'd always thought it would happen—with caution, control, and timing. No, this was the headfirst, heart-wrecking kind. The kind that made him want to rewrite every plan he'd made for his future just to make space for her.

Especially when someone new might already be on the way.

His gaze drifted to her stomach. Flat and tan. Beautiful. He knew she hadn't had her period since they'd been back together. Nearly three weeks. A flicker of hope stirred deep inside him.

Could she be pregnant?

The thought didn't scare him. It thrilled him.

The idea of Dani—his Dani—carrying their child, her body

rounded with new life, her laughter and the sounds of a baby's coo filling their home...

His chest tightened with emotion.

She caught him staring and raised an eyebrow. "You're looking at me like I just grew a second head."

He cleared his throat and gave her a crooked smile. "Just wondering if we might be welcoming a third crewmember soon."

Her brow furrowed. "Is that your way of suggesting we adopt a cat?"

He barked a laugh. "God, no. I enjoy breathing—and remaining in one piece. Cats hate me."

She smiled but tilted her head, watching him with curious eyes. "Then what?"

He hesitated. Should he bring it up now? Or wait until tonight?

Dani leaned forward, studying his face. "You're fidgeting."

"I do not fidget."

"You fidget when you're nervous."

"I'm not—" He paused. Sighed. "Okay. Maybe I am a little nervous."

She set the bowl of oranges aside and shifted closer. "Talk to me."

He drew in a breath and reached for her hand. "Dani, these last few weeks... they've been the best of my life. I don't say that lightly. You know me. I don't—romanticize—or I didn't until I met you. Now, it seems to be all I do."

She giggled and nodded. A tiny smile curved her lips as she studied his face.

"I've never felt this way about anyone. And I've never wanted a future with someone the way I want one with you," he continued.

Her eyes widened slightly. Her lips parted.

"So, I need to ask you something. Two things, actually."

She didn't speak, but her grip on his hand tightened.

He reached into the pocket of his shorts and pulled out a small velvet box. "First," he said, opening it to reveal a delicate diamond and emerald eternity ring nestled in the folds. "Will you marry me?"

Her breath caught. Her eyes filled with tears.

"And second," he said gently, "do you think you might be pregnant?"

Her silence stretched into stunned stillness… then broke with a laugh that was half-sob, half-disbelief.

"Oh my God," she whispered. "You really don't waste time."

He smiled. "I've wasted enough. I want you, Dani. All of you. For the rest of my life. And if there's a little heartbeat joining us soon…" He touched her flat belly with reverence. "…that just makes this moment even more perfect."

Her cheeks flushed with a delicate pink. "Yes," she whispered. "To the first. And… maybe to the second. I was going to get a pregnancy test the next time we stopped."

He leaned in, kissed her lips that tasted of tangy orange, and wrapped his arms around her.

"We'll do even better, I'll make an appointment for you to see a doctor—after we are married. I don't want to wait until spring," he groaned, kissing her neck and sliding his hand under her top to cup her breast.

"Anchor. We need to put the anchors out," she breathed, twisting the steering wheel and pulling back on the throttle.

CHAPTER 17

The aluminum dinghy scraped gently against the dock. Dani jumped out to tie it off before Alexandros could. She still hummed with a pleasant buzz from their brief detour—because that man could melt her bones with a single touch.

Demetrius waited for them at the boathouse. The rhythmic lapping of water against the wooden pilings was a steady counterpoint to his restless pacing as they idled closer. His face was unreadable until his gaze locked onto hers—then shifted as he caught the flash of the diamond and emerald ring. A slow smile spread across his face, his eyes crinkling at the corners with approval.

"I'll warn you now that I've upgraded security since you were last here," he greeted in a dry voice. "Apparently, our perimeter can be breached with a stolen tin can and a determined woman."

Dani laughed. "You forgot 'resourceful.' I borrowed the dinghy. Borrowed. Big difference."

Alexandros groaned behind her. "Please don't encourage her."

"I wouldn't dream of it," Demetrius replied, though the sparkle in his eyes said otherwise. "But it did make the case for a few new cameras."

"Just so you know, you'll probably end up with footage of me skinny-dipping off the back deck," Dani called out over her shoulder.

Demetrius coughed—into his hand, barely hiding a smirk.

Alexandros tripped on the dock ladder and scowled first at her before he turned a warning glare to Demetrius.

Dani grinned.

"I told you she was going to be trouble," Demetrius chuckled before his humor faded. "You have an unexpected visitor. She arrived an hour ago."

Alexandros straightened, the muscle in his jaw tightening. "Who?"

"Gina Rossi."

The name hung in the air like a cork from a bottle no one wanted to open.

Dani caught the briefest flicker of distaste in Demetrius's otherwise professional demeanor. But it was nothing compared to the steel that snapped into Alexandros's spine.

"Well," he said with the warmth of a glacier, "that explains the headache I didn't know I had."

"Old friend?"

Demetrius's mouth twitched. "In her dreams."

Alexandros turned to her. "Why don't you go upstairs and get cleaned up? I'll—"

"Nope," she said breezily, cutting him off. "I think I'd like to meet this surprise guest. After all, I live here now too, don't I? It wouldn't be proper if I was rude." She gave him a smile that was just a little too sweet. "Besides, I'm dying to see what kind of woman gives my fiancé indigestion at the mere mention of her name."

Demetrius choked again.

Alexandros gave her a pained look. Not exactly pleading, but definitely... wary.

Which, of course, only made her more curious.

Hand in hand, they ascended the wide stone steps. The sun was beginning to set, painting the villa in golden hues—and apparently, it brought the drama with it.

Dani let go of Alexandros's hand just as a tall, breathtakingly beautiful blonde swept out of the double doors onto the terrace. Dani's nose wrinkled when she caught the scent of expensive perfume and entitlement.

So this is the mysterious Gina Rossi.

Gina released a high, girly squeal that made Dani's molars ache, and launched herself at Alexandros like a heat-seeking missile.

"Alexandros! Darling! Did you miss me? I've missed you. Paris was simply boring without you. And what have you said to poor Vito? He's wallowing in self-pity at the gaming tables in Morocco like his best friend has died," she cried, throwing her arms around his neck before Dani could so much as blink.

The vision of talons on a chalkboard changed to a red haze when Gina clamped her blood-red lips to Alexandros's before he could respond. The lip lock was a full-on, no-holds-barred, suck his tonsils out kiss. Gina kissed him as if it was her audition for a soap opera— and her big break.

Dani froze. For one wild second, she thought she was hallucinating. But no, that was definitely Gina's mouth plastered to her fiancé's.

Alexandros peeled her off with the enthusiasm of someone removing a slug from their shirt.

"Gina," he said, his voice flat. "What are you doing here?"

She pouted. "I told your assistant I was coming. I thought we could catch up." Then, as if noticing Dani for the first time, she turned and gave her a bright, insincere smile. "And you must be…?"

Dani smiled sweetly, stepping forward and threading her arm through Alexandros's with lazy familiarity.

"Dani Collins," she greeted in a cheerful voice. "Fiancée."

Gina blinked at the ring Dani flashed. Dani could feel the other woman's scrutiny as she ran her gaze from head to toe all the way to her bone marrow. Dani recognized the look instantly—the same one designer sales associates gave her when she walked in wearing greasy overalls, moments before trying to usher her out.

"Oh," Gina said with a plastic smile. "How… quaint."

Behind Gina, Dani caught Demetrius's dry murmur: "Gina is Vito's stepsister."

Aha.

Jealousy flared, hot and unexpected, but Dani didn't flinch. Instead, she leaned in and pressed a kiss to Alexandros's cheek.

His arm wrapped around her, and he started to turn his head towards her, but she stopped him with a caress to his cheek.

Leaning closer to his ear, she whispered, loud enough for everyone to hear, "I'm not kissing you again until you brush your teeth."

Alexandros stifled a laugh.

Dani patted his chest, dragging her palm down with slow, lingering possession before she pulled away. "I'm going to shower," she tossed out with a bright, fake smile. "You two have fun catching up. But if you need anything, darling, just shout. I'm sure Demetrius would be happy to help take out the trash."

With one last sweet smile, she turned and sauntered toward the stairs.

Her heart was pounding, but her face was calm.

Dani knew Gina was trouble the moment she strutted out like the villa was her catwalk. But *she* had a wrench, a blowtorch, and a wicked imagination—and she could think of at least twelve different ways to hide a body on the villa grounds without messing up the landscaping.

Let Gina try something again.

Dani Collins wasn't going anywhere.

And neither was her man.

ALEXANDROS LOOKED with disapproval at Gina when he noticed the flash of irritation change to calculation. He had seen that look far too many times when the young woman wanted something and had been told no. He'd been on the receiving end of that look before. But this time, it mattered. She was trying to drive a wedge between him and Dani. He wouldn't allow it—not even for the sake of peace.

"Our families—our fathers—" Gina began, her mouth drawn into a practiced pout that probably still worked on half the men in Rome.

He stepped away when she lifted her hand to touch him again. Her lips tightened, and another flash of annoyance swept across her face.

"Alexandros," she pouted, giving him a puppy-eyed look of hurt.

He shook his head, his patience nearing an end. "They were drunk in a den when we were kids and still laugh about it over dinner," he said flatly. "It was not a blood oath. There was no agreement. Formal, informal, imagined, or otherwise."

"But… they both want it. If you turn your back on us, you'll be breaking with tradition!"

"No, Gina. I'm starting my own." He stared her down. "With Dani."

He knew instantly that mentioning Dani's name had broken through Gina's defenses; a subtle shift in her eyes betrayed the fracture. Her polished facade slipped, revealing the ice beneath.

Her voice turned cold, bitter. "If you want to slum it with a grease-stained mechanic—yes, Vito told me exactly who she is—don't be surprised when she bores you; or worse, embarrasses you in front of half of the world."

Instead of being offended, he chuckled—only fueling Gina's rage. Gina had no idea *who* Dani really was, nor the power behind her. He saw no point in continuing the argument when all he wanted was to join Dani upstairs, where the warm steam from the shower enveloped them. The image of Dani, water cascading over her smooth skin, sent a jolt of excitement through him; his blood rushed south.

He gave Gina a look weighted with finality. His stare conveyed the gravity of her actions, making her realize her mistake.

"Alexandros? Are you serious? You-you would choose that-that *nobody* over me?" Gina demanded.

Her hand lifted to her throat as she stared back at him in disbelief. All the expensive tutors and polished manners couldn't mask the entitled, spoiled child lurking beneath the surface of the younger woman.

Her entitlement radiated outwards, a palpable wave of self-importance that clashed sharply with Dani's gentle humility. Gina didn't care about anyone else. She was utterly self-absorbed, unconcerned with the feelings or needs of others.

She loved the idea of him—the status, the money, the photo ops, the lifestyle. She belonged to a world he'd gladly left behind. Dani was his future.

"Goodbye, Gina," he said. "Demetrius will show you out."

Alexandros felt the tension bleed out of him as Demetrius escorted a stunned Gina out of the villa and to her car. He breathed a sigh of relief when the front doors of the villa closed behind the two, cutting off Gina's furious threats.

A slow, devilish grin curved his lips. Now, to do what he had been fantasizing about. Rubbing his hands together, he exited the salon and climbed the stairs. His heart already pounding for an entirely different reason as he neared his and Dani's bedroom.

He entered the room, closing and locking the door behind him. The bathroom door was ajar, the ambient light casting a halo into the dim room. He heard the shower.

A low chuckle slipped from him when he heard Dani's voice.

"Touch him again, and I'll hide your body in one of the villa's ten thousand olive urns. No jury would convict me."

A pause.

"Oh, and if he tries to kiss me before he brushes his teeth, I'll bite his tongue. No, no. I can't do that. He does such wonderful things with his tongue. I love it when he—"

The sound of Dani's curse followed by a low moan of desire pulled him forward. There was something sexy in a woman who could make death threats sound adorable.

He shed his clothes quickly—shoes, shirt, shorts, briefs—then padded into the bathroom. Steam wrapped around him, caressing his skin.

Dani stood in the shower, her back to the tiled wall, red curls plastered to her shoulders, one foot propped lazily on the small ledge as she—. His breath caught as he watched, mesmerized, as her hand caressed the sensitive spot between her legs.

She looked up and saw him—and her entire body flooded with intense desire. She wanted him—but not with Gina's lipstick and scent on him.

"You better not even think about kissing me until you brush those teeth, Romeo."

He didn't say a word. He just grabbed his toothbrush and the toothpaste and calmly went to work scrubbing his teeth like a man on a mission.

She watched, her eyes sparkling with invitation as she continued to rub the hidden jewel he loved to tease with his tongue. His gaze never wavered as she traced a path from her belly to her breast with her free hand, cupping the soft globe. Her eyelids drooped languidly, her lips parting in a slow, sexy smile that hinted at untold desires.

"You're brushing while naked. That's oddly… erotic. Still not sure it's enough. I think I need something… more."

He spat, rinsed, and flicked water from his mouth like a wet lion, then carefully replaced the toothbrush on the corner shelf.

His gaze lifted to hers. Gleamed.

Challenge accepted.

Dani's smile faltered into something softer. Hotter.

She extended her arm in silent invitation.

"It took you long enough to get rid of her," she murmured, when he opened the glass door and stepped into the shower. She reached over and picked up the soap, lathering it on the washcloth before she began gliding it over his body. Her lips pursed as she followed a line of suds running down his chest. "I can't stand the thought of you smelling like designer desperation."

"I want you, Dani—only you. Always you," he murmured, his voice low and thick as her hands traced down his torso.

Her touch was unhurried, reverent, and deliberate.

Her lips curved into a satisfied smile when his cock twitched against her thigh. He leaned forward, relishing in the feel of Dani's slick skin against his and the warmth of the water coursed over his shoulders as if they were standing under a waterfall. He kissed the pulse on her neck, running his tongue over it.

"You missed a spot," he growled.

Her hand slid lower.

Then lower still.

And suddenly, the playful tease melted into something darker. Needier. She dropped the soap when he suddenly cradled one hand on the back of her neck. He slid his other hand under her thigh as he pulled her up against him. Her arms wrapped around his shoulders, her legs around his waist, slick skin against slick skin as he pressed her back to the warm tile.

His mouth claimed hers—fierce, hot, possessive.

She moaned against him, her hips tilting just enough, guiding him in as he surged forward, claiming her in one deep, demanding stroke.

Her head fell back.

"Where else do you like my tongue?" he asked, voice ragged.

"Everywhere... Oh, God, everywhere," she gasped.

This is what he loved about Dani. She made him lose control. It wouldn't matter if they made love a million times. He would never get enough of her.

He gripped her thighs, rocking his hips in powerful thrusts, each one a vow. Each fervent kiss was a promise of the future they would have together.

Alexandros poured everything he had into the beautiful woman in his arms. He wasn't just making love to her—he was anchoring them both, forging a bond no storm could break.

Dani's body clenched around him, her release rippling through her. She released a muffled cry of ecstasy against his neck as her body convulsed. The feel of her silky channel, squeezing him, was too much. His legs trembled, forcing him to lean forward. He pressed into her, too weak to stop himself from melting into the heat of her body.

"I want to lose myself in you—again and again. Every second with you is an eternity I crave," he murmured in Greek, the words too raw to say in English. "I love you, Dani. I won't ever let you leave me again. Never, Danika. You must promise never to leave me again."

"I promise. We're in this together. I love you. I'll love you forever," she murmured, threading her fingers through his hair and holding him to her as if she would never let him go.

She already knew.

She was his.

And nothing, not a thousand Gina Rossis or even the uncertainty of life, could ever change that.

EPILOGUE

*L*aughter shimmered through the warm evening air like champagne bubbles, floating across the terrace of the Kallistratos villa. Strings of fairy lights glowed in the tropical shrubbery, casting a soft shimmer over linen-covered tables and tumbling flower arrangements in soft pinks, creams, and coral. Guests mingled beneath the stars, their silhouettes flickering in the glow of candlelit lanterns hung from the pergola and carved wall niches.

Alexandros stood at the terrace's edge, the sea breeze tugging at his tuxedo jacket—but it was the vision beyond the archway that stole his breath.

Dani.

She was in his father's arms, her ivory silk wedding gown shimmering like moonlight against her sun-kissed skin. Christos twirled her expertly, her laughter ringing out like music, as the soft hum of a bouzouki and violin played an old love song across the stone-paved courtyard.

Alexandros's heart squeezed with the force of everything he felt for her.

"Not bad for a mechanic," Stuart said beside him, swirling a glass of dark red wine with a satisfied grunt. His cheeks were rosy, and his tie hung loose around his neck.

Alexandros frowned, startled from his reverie. "Excuse me?"

Stuart chuckled, nodding toward Dani with a wistful smile. "She's glowing. You did that. So... thank you."

Alexandros blinked. "For what?"

Stuart dropped into a cushioned chair and leaned back, one hand folded over his full stomach like a man savoring a good life. His silver brows relaxed, his eyes locked on his granddaughter with pride so deep it seemed to anchor him to the earth. "For loving her just the way she is."

Alexandros looked back at Dani. The sweep of her dress. The flash of her grin as she teased his father. The wild red curls pinned with jeweled combs, half slipping free from the elegant chignon.

His voice was quiet. Honest. "That's the easy part."

He paused, drawing in a deep breath. They hadn't shared that she was expecting yet. Dani had wanted to keep it between themselves until they knew for sure. The doctor had confirmed it yesterday.

His eyes burned as he thought of the ultrasound and the first faint photo of their child. He kept a copy of the scan tucked in his wallet.

"I'm the lucky one."

Stuart snorted. "I'll remind you of that the first time you find a carburetor next to your croissant."

"I can always help her put it together."

Laughter rumbled between them before Stuart waved him off with a grin and raised his glass in approval.

As the song came to a close, Alexandros stepped forward, drawn to his new wife like the tide to the shore. She saw him the moment he moved, her eyes lighting up like she'd waited her whole life for him. Christos released her with a kiss to her hand, and she drifted into Alexandros's arms.

"Everything alright?" she asked, wrapping her arms around his neck.

"It is for me." He glanced around, his lips twitching as he paused on the silhouette of a man standing off to the side. "Though I'm not sure my brother is feeling quite as celebratory."

She arched an eyebrow. "Theo?"

He nodded discreetly toward the edge of the garden.

Dani followed his gaze, her lips parting with a soft 'oh' before laughter bubbled out of her.

Theo stood rigid beside the stone balustrade, clearly trying to disappear behind a potted lemon tree while Gina Rossi—draped in a crimson gown so tight it could double as shrink wrap—chatted animatedly to his shoulder.

"I think he'll survive," Dani said, still laughing. "He's quick on his feet. Besides, he owes me for not warning me you snore."

"I do not snore."

"You purr like a sinusy dragon."

"Only when you over exhaust me with your demands," he countered, before he added, "And in case you didn't know it, I'm not the only dragon with a cold."

He buried his face in her neck, chuckling when she scoffed at his suggestion that she snored. He pressed a kiss to the delicate skin just below her ear. His hand slid instinctively to her stomach, still marveling at the hidden treasure growing inside her.

She giggled, catching his hand. "I'm fine. It was just this morning so far. If I'm lucky, it will be the only round of praying to the porcelain gods I have."

His chest tightened at the memory. He still hadn't fully recovered from seeing her so pale, curled up in his arms. He would have traded anything—his fortune, his company, his name—if he could have taken the sickness from her.

"You were white as a sheet and shaking," he murmured against her skin. "It scared me."

Her hand rose to cradle his cheek. "It's just a reminder of the miracle growing inside me," she said gently. "I'd go through it all again. For this. For us."

He kissed her then, long and slow, letting the taste of her settle deep in his bones.

When he finally pulled back, mischief danced in his eyes.

"Do you think we've stayed long enough to sneak away without sparking a family incident?"

She tilted her head, pretending to consider it, then whispered, "I know where this cute little dinghy is tied up."

His grin was wicked.

Seconds later, they were slipping through the side gate, Dani barefoot and radiant, their laughter trailing behind them as they dashed down the moonlit path toward the boathouse.

From the terrace, Stuart watched them go, shaking his head with a smile.

"I wonder how far they get before Demetrius sends out the cavalry?"

Christos lifted his glass. "Not far—but they'll be discreet. I wonder how long it will be before they tell us she is pregnant," he chuckled.

LATER THAT NIGHT, the soft hum of the engines vibrated gently beneath her as the *Kallistratos Challenge* glided through the moonlit waters of the Aegean Sea. They were going to spend the next month cruising the Mediterranean coast. The yacht's polished decks and gleaming hull were a far cry from the creaky charm of her old trawler.

Part of her still missed the familiar comfort of the aged interior and sun-bleached ropes. But as she lay back against the rich cotton sheets in the master stateroom, her fingers trailing along the broad muscles of Alexandros's bare back, Dani knew with quiet certainty:

This was her life now.

Not because of the yacht, or the headlines, or the quiet ring of protection against the world. But because of the man resting his cheek against her stomach, whispering to their unborn son in a husky mix of Greek and English, his voice tinged with both laughter and gentle scolding.

"Be kind to your mama, little lion. She already has to put up with me. Don't make her sick tomorrow, alright?" He paused, pressing another kiss just above her navel. "She's very, very precious to us. It is our job to take good care of her."

Dani smiled tenderly, her fingers gliding through his silky hair, massaging gently, while sliding her other hand to rest over the place he had just kissed. A warm flutter answered beneath her palm, as if their son had heard him.

She blinked, surprised by the sting in her eyes. Tears blurred the edges of the stateroom—the soft lamps, the slow dance of shadows on the walls, the elegant carved wood and marble. But it wasn't the space or the moment that brought the ache.

It was because of her dream.

Last night, she had seen them. Her parents.

And she thought she finally understood.

In her dream, they had been holding each other, arm-in-arm, younger than she ever remembered—her mother's laugh ringing like wind chimes, her father standing strong and tall, his green eyes full of love. They had been walking through a garden she didn't recognize but somehow knew. The grass sparkled like dew-dusted emeralds, and diamond lights shimmered through trees that swayed as if stirred by memory, not wind.

When they turned... they looked at her.

And smiled.

Not a farewell, but a quiet reassurance that everything would be alright.

She hadn't wanted to wake. But when she did, the deep, aching hole in her heart felt full—for the first time since the accident.

Because love didn't end. Not even in death.

A tear slid down her cheek.

He lifted his head, brows drawing together, his hand rising to caress her cheek. "Dani?" Alexandros's voice was suddenly taut with concern. "What's wrong, Agapi *mou*?"

She looked down at him, his stormy eyes shadowed with worry, and her heart clenched at the depth of his love.

"Nothing," she whispered, brushing his hair back from his face. "Nothing's wrong. Not even a little."

She cradled his face between her hands. "Everything is perfect."

Relief flooded his expression. He rose over her, his body warm and solid, his arms braced on either side of her as his lips brushed hers with reverence.

"Yes," he whispered, his voice low and rough as he kissed her again, his eyes locked to hers, the truth of his love blazing between them. "It is. Just like you."

And in that moment—wrapped in his arms, their child safe within her, and the stars spilling like diamonds across the dark sea—Dani knew what forever felt like.

She was home. In Alexandros's arms, and he in hers. They were exactly where they were meant to be.

Ready for more?

Read on to discover S.E. Smith's next release!

She was fated to be the champion of those in need...

Dalla Bogadottir knew the day would come when she would be awakened again. When she hears the soft plea on the wind, she doesn't hesitate to answer the call-to-arms. What she didn't expect was how much the world has changed since she last woke.

Sheik Nasser Al-Rashid and his brother, Musad, have made a vow to protect their kingdom and their people no matter the cost. On a desperate mission, they are caught in a trap—and it seems their death is inescapable.

In the heat of battle, a legendary warrior from the scrolls of time appears—but is she real or an imposter? Could she have been sent by their enemies to pit brother against brother and undermine their rule? As the mystery deepens, Nasser and Musad decide to guard Dalla against those who would use her or kill her to gain power.

Can a legendary woman thought only to be a myth capture the hearts of her royal guards, or will time run out for her as she faces her greatest battle yet... the one for love?

Coming Soon

ADDITIONAL BOOKS

If you loved this story by me (Susan aka S.E. Smith) please leave a review! My websites are https://sesmithfl.com and https://sesmithya.com. Be sure to sign up for my newsletter to hear about new releases. Find your favorite way to keep in touch here: https://sesmithfl.com/contact-me/

RECOMMENDED READING ORDER LISTS:
https://sesmithfl.com/reading-list-by-events/
https://sesmithfl.com/reading-list-by-series/

MY GENRES:

Contemporary / Romance
Girls from the Street
She was born on the streets; he was born to rule.
Street smart. Heart strong. Unstoppable. A heart-pounding, emotional series where ordinary women become extraordinary, and love proves the strongest weapon of all.

S.E. SMITH SIGNATURE ROMANCE

<u>HEART AND SOULS SERIES</u>: *Passion. Power. Heart.*
Breathtaking settings. Unforgettable characters. Sizzling chemistry.

Science Fiction / Romance
Dragon Lords of Valdier
It all started with a king who crashed on Earth, desperately hurt. He inadvertently discovered a species that would save his own.

Curizan Warrior
The Curizans have a secret, kept even from their closest allies, but even they are not immune to the draw of a little known species from an isolated planet called Earth.

Marastin Dow Warriors
The Marastin Dow are reviled and feared for their ruthlessness, but not all want to live a life of murder. Some wait for just the right time to escape....

Sarafin Warriors
A hilariously ridiculous human family who happen to be quite formidable... and a secret hidden on Earth. The origin of the Sarafin species is more than it seems. Those cat-shifting aliens won't know what hit them!

Dragonlings of Valdier Novellas
The Valdier, Sarafin, and Curizan Lords had children who just cannot stop getting into trouble! There is nothing as cute or funny as magical, shapeshifting kids, and nothing as heartwarming as family.

Cosmos' Gateway
Cosmos created a portal between his lab and the warriors of Prime. Discover new worlds, new species, and outrageous adventures as secrets are unravelled and bridges are crossed.

The Alliance
When Earth received its first visitors from space, the planet was thrown into a panicked chaos. The Trivators came to bring Earth into the Alliance of Star

Systems, but now they must take control to prevent the humans from destroying themselves. No one was prepared for how the humans will affect the Trivators, though, starting with a family of three sisters....

Lords of Kassis
It began with a random abduction and a stowaway, and yet, somehow, the Kassisans knew the humans were coming long before now. The fate of more than one world hangs in the balance, and time is not always linear....

Zion Warriors
Time travel, epic heroics, and love beyond measure. Sci-fi adventures with heart and soul, laughter, and awe-inspiring discovery...

Rings of Power
Powerful mages. Epic love. Every world holds a new chance to rewrite destiny.

Paranormal / Fantasy / Romance
Magic, New Mexico
Within New Mexico is a small town named Magic, an... unusual town, to say the least. With no beginning and no end, spanning genres, authors, and universes, hilarity and drama combine to keep you on the edge of your seat!

Spirit Pass
There is a physical connection between two times. Follow the stories of those who travel back and forth. These westerns are as wild as they come!

Second Chance
Stand-alone worlds featuring a woman who remembers her own death. Fiery and mysterious, these books will steal your heart.

More Than Human
Long ago there was a war on Earth between shifters and humans. Humans lost, and today they know they will become extinct if something is not done....

The Fairy Tale Series
A twist on your favorite fairy tales!

A Seven Kingdoms Tale
Long ago, a strange entity came to the Seven Kingdoms to conquer and feed on their life force. It found a host, and she battled it within her body for centuries while destruction and devastation surrounded her. Our story begins when the end is near, and a portal is opened....

Epic Science Fiction / Action Thrillers
Project Gliese 581G
An international team leave Earth to investigate a mysterious object in our solar system that was clearly made by someone, someone who isn't from Earth. Discover new worlds and conflicts in a sci-fi adventure sure to become your favorite!

New Adult / Young Adult
Breaking Free
A journey that will challenge everything she has ever believed about herself as danger reveals itself in sudden, heart-stopping moments.

The Dust Series
Fragments of a comet hit Earth, and Dust wakes to discover the world as he knew it is gone. It isn't the only thing that has changed, though, so has Dust...

ABOUT THE AUTHOR

S.E. Smith is an *internationally acclaimed, New York Times* **and** *USA TODAY Bestselling* author of science fiction, romance, fantasy, paranormal, and contemporary works for adults, young adults, and children. She enjoys writing a wide variety of genres that pull her readers into worlds that take them away.